EXILE'S HUNTER

ALIEN MATES: PLANET EXILE

KATE RUDOLPH

ABOUT EXILE'S HUNTER

Guerran is no place for pretty human women, but tough-as-nails Kenzie will walk through hell to find her abducted sister.

When her search puts her in Mad's path she isn't sure whether she should kiss him or stab him. He's as handsome as the devil, and practically a giant with a huge... axe. The aliens on Guerran are criminals and she can't trust him. But she needs a guide and Mad is her only hope. She certainly can't fall for him. No matter how much he makes her yearn.

Guerran is the dumping ground for Kru'dari criminals and Mad has been ekeing out a life there for six years. But when Kenzie appears, suddenly he's thinking about the future and one word keeps ringing in his head.

Mate.

He will protect her from the worst Guerran has to offer as she throws herself into its darkest corners in her desperate search for her sister. And he'll fight an Exile King to keep her safe, but can he convince the human woman to take a chance on him once the battle is through?

PROLOGUE

Six Years Ago

The cell around him was pure cement and the bars were unbreakable. Madn Damari knew the stories of the jails of Krudare. Everyone did. No one escaped. Ever. The king's justice was swift for anyone who tried.

At first he'd paced in the small space allotted to him. He was fortunate enough to have his own cell. On his way into the facility, he'd passed by cells filled to the brim with the dregs of society, and the stench nearly overwhelmed him.

He was one of those dregs now.

He couldn't regret it. He knew his duty as a soldier and as Kru'dari. His honor was worth more than his freedom. He only hoped he would be strong enough to keep believing that once the judge passed down his final sentence.

Boots pounded down the hallway, nearly drowning out the tippy-tap of daintier shoes. But Mad heard the footsteps, and he recognized them. He shot up from the bench and crossed the two steps to the bars. It only took a moment for his sister to appear.

"You have ten minutes," the guard grunted at her before stepping back.

They wouldn't have true privacy, but he stood far enough away that they could speak quietly enough to not be overheard.

"Oh, Mad." Taiana reached her hand into the cell and clutched at him. She was everything a Kru'dari lady should be—regal, poised, and nearly as tall as him, but wearing a flowy dress that hid her bulk. Her skin was pale and her hands uncalloused. She spent her days working with the upper echelon of the king's government.

He'd been a lowly soldier.

"No need for tears," he said, putting as much confidence into his voice as he could muster. "We've hours yet before the judgement is passed."

She sucked in a shaky breath and pulled her hand away.

Mad's heart sank. Taiana couldn't hide her

emotions from him. She'd never learned the trick. And the fear and anguish he saw on her made his heart crack in two. The guilt, though—that emotion stole away his hope and drowned it in the sea.

Taiana straightened her shoulders and fixed her expression. He'd seen soldiers look softer before charging into battle. "Arbyn spoke with the judge."

Mad growled. He didn't want his sister's slimy fiancé anywhere near his case.

She glared at him for a minute before steeling her resolve once more. "He pulled as many strings as he could. Execution was *strongly* considered. But you're not to be killed."

"Exile?" His heart sank, and he pulled at the energy that ran through Krudare. Called the Fount, it was the source of his people's prosperity. Energy ran through the planet, and all Kru'dari could access it. It made them stronger, faster, and sharper than anyone else.

And being separated from that power was supposed to be a fate worse than death.

Taiana nodded.

"How long?" He gripped the bar tight and wished he had the strength to bend it. But he could drink the Fount dry and the bars wouldn't move an inch.

"Indefinite. Arbyn can't work miracles." She looked away.

It was for the best. She didn't see the way he snarled. It sounded to him as if Arbyn had done *nothing*. Yes, execution had been on the table. But the king didn't like the spectacle. He far preferred to send his problems away. Indefinite exile had always been the most likely outcome.

"Have Mother and Father been to see you?" she asked once she'd collected herself.

"Not since the trial." The look of utter disgust on his parents' faces should have hurt him, but there was no way to please them. They'd always had a favorite child, and she was standing on the right side of the bars.

"I'll speak with them," Taiana promised.

"Don't waste your breath." She might need them one day now that he wouldn't be there to protect her. "Listen, about Arb—"

"Time's up," the guard announced, stepping close. "Say your goodbyes."

His sister didn't cry and he was glad. If tears fell from her eyes, he wouldn't have been able to keep his composure. She reached into the cell one more time and clasped his hand. "Stay strong. I'll work every day to get you a pardon. I'll bring you home."

The guard led her away but sent a scowl Mad's way, reminding him that his sister might believe in him, but no one else did.

He didn't expect to sleep that night, but there was a funny taste to his evening meal, and he succumbed to darkness not long after.

He woke with a gasp and sucked in heavy breaths. His lungs were on fire and his guts felt like they'd been torn out. He writhed on the ground and tried to figure out what was going on.

Was he being executed? Had the judge changed his mind?

But there was dirt under his fingers rather than hard cement, and when he finally pried his eyes open, he saw a dark night sky studded with stars.

Guerran.

He was on Guerran, Krudare's planet of exiles.

And he'd been ripped from the Fount.

Mad had heard the stories of what it felt like to lose a connection to the Fount, but he'd never let himself believe it could happen to him. The Kru'dari had evolved to need the excess energy the Fount provided. Without it, their bodies eventually starved.

Or they found other ways to feed.

A boot kicked him in the stomach, and Mad realized he wasn't alone. Then a hand clamped on his neck and dragged him to his feet. His attacker was another Kru'dari, and his eyes seemed to glow red in the pale light.

But that must have been a trick of the light.

"Fresh meat." The exile grinned.

Mad risked a look around and saw he and his attacker were alone. He didn't know why he'd been abandoned like this. He was almost certain there was supposed to be some sort of orientation for life on Guerran.

Instead he had a trial by fire.

And he wasn't about to lose.

The Kru'dari who had him was strong, but Mad was skilled. He kicked him where it hurt and jerked back when his attacker loosened his grip. Mad was groggy, weak, and unarmed, but he wasn't going to die in his first hours on Guerran. He refused.

He charged his attacker and took him to the ground, letting out all of his frustration with each angry punch. And as his fists unleashed their fury, something happened.

His gut-wrenching pain faded. Energy seeped into his bones. And he almost felt whole.

He pulled back before he killed the man. He was an exile, but he wasn't a murderer.

He heard rowdy men getting closer and clenched his fists. The energy within him was weak, but it was *there*. It wasn't the Fount, but it meant Guerran wasn't a death sentence.

It would be if the rowdy crowd found him, though.

"New guy, over here." A Kru'dari in dark clothes with his hair tied back beckoned him to the shadows.

Mad didn't move. "Show yourself."

The man stepped into the light. He had a scar on his cheek and blond hair. He was tall, even for a Kru'dari. "My name is Jaek. I mean you no harm. Now grab your bag before we're discovered."

Mad looked toward the ground where Jaek had nodded, and, sure enough, there was a cloth sack lying there. Mad looked inside and saw some clothes, a wallet full of credits, and a leather pouch brimming with power. He pulled it out in confusion.

Jaek hissed. "Hide that if you know what's good for you. A Pitcher is worth more than both our lives in this territory."

A Pitcher. A fragment of the Fount's power preserved for long travel. It was the only way Kru'-dari could leave their home planet. And even then, the Pitchers couldn't preserve power for long.

Mad stuffed it back in the bag and slung a strap over his shoulder. He followed Jaek away from the scene of his attack. He hoped the exile didn't kill him.

But given his welcome on Guerran, Mad wasn't sure how long he'd want to survive.

1

Some days Mad dreamed he was back on Krudare. He'd have dinner with his family to celebrate his newest military promotion. He'd play with his young nephew and show him how to slip into the kitchen and steal cookies when the servants weren't looking.

And he'd punch the living shit out of his sister's husband.

There was no dreaming today. His fist sank into the hard flesh of his opponent's abdomen and the man doubled over with a grunt. This wasn't a fight for energy. This was payback.

"Do it again and Jadirel won't send *me* next time," Mad warned, shoving the man away and taking a step back. They were in the middle of the market in Jadirel's territory.

Orion, the biggest city on Guerran, was split up into hundreds of territories ruled by exile kings. There were no laws except for what the kings decreed, and surviving one day to another wasn't guaranteed.

Oron scuttled back, blue eyes wide and mouth hanging open. "I didn't do anything!" he protested. It came out in a wheeze.

Mad shrugged. He left Oron where he was. The exile was new to Guerran. He'd arrived with the last batch of criminals and served in a different territory. Oron was little more than a boy. A few years ago, Mad might have pitied him or tried help, but he wasn't a fool anymore.

He had the scars from more than one lesson learned.

His energy was low, and he wanted to crawl back to his quarters and sleep for a week. He'd fought in the pit the night before, desperate for the energy winning a fight would give him. He hated the fights, but there was no way to get a Pitcher from Krudare. If he didn't fight, he'd have to fuck, and he didn't trust a Kru'dari not to stab him while he slept.

Kru'dari energy was scare on Guerran. They generated an excess when emotions ran high, which made the fights popular. When Mad entered the pit, he usually won.

But everyone had an off night. And to make matters worse, he had to report back to Jadirel.

The streets of the market were dusty, making his eyes water. Jadirel's territory was falling into disrepair. The exile king didn't want to waste labor on rebuilding crumbling roads or constructing new buildings, so the people in the territory had done what they could for three years. The roof of Mad's own quarters threatened to collapse any day, and he knew of more than one family that lived in a house without all of its walls.

There was no love for Jadirel in his territory. But he was a jealous king and he didn't let his people leave.

Especially not his soldiers.

Mad passed a market stall and paused when he saw the flyer posted on the flaking wood. There was a picture of a young man with dark hair and a cheerful smile.

FUGITIVE

WANTED BY THE KING

IF DISCOVERED DELIVER TO THE GREEN ZONE

REWARD CONSIDERED

He'd seen dozens of flyers like that in his six

years on the planet and ignored most of them. Guerran was a land of exiles, and no honest Kru'dari would choose to land there.

But Kru'dari weren't the only people on the planet. The city was made up of beings from all across space.

And more than a few fugitives.

Outside the Green Zone, which was controlled by the Kru'dari king, Guerran was a lawless place. And fugitives from nearby systems, and the especially desperate from Krudare, tested their luck in its narrow alleys.

Reward considered.

Those two words echoed in Mad's head, and he tore the flyer from the post and folded it up before stuffing it in his pocket. Every year, the king pardoned some exiles on Guerran. There was no specific number or reason.

But perhaps returning a fugitive might earn Mad the favor he needed to return home.

His nephew was nearly two years old now. He'd missed his birth. Not to mention his sister's wedding to Arbyn. His family survived without him, but he wanted back in.

A ship zoomed overhead, its engines loud enough to make Mad wince and remind him that a pardon wasn't his only way off of Guerran. The guards did little to stop exiles from leaving for other planets.

But those who chose to leave could never be pardoned. They were as good as dead to everyone back home.

Mad had to put thoughts of a pardon and home out of his mind as he approached Jadirel's palace. *This* building wasn't in disrepair. The walls outside gleamed, and colored glass covered the narrow windows in swirls of red, purple, and blue. The entry was a stone archway with door made of solid metal, as thick and tall as two men. It was wide enough to let four Kru'dari warriors brimming with armor and weapons walk in side by side.

And inside, the palace was even grander.

Mad walked through a narrow hall, the walls carved in white stone, the carvings depicting Kru'-dari myths and legend. The hall was easily defensible. No army could storm Jadirel's fortress without being picked off in this passageway.

Mad nodded to the two guards standing at their posts. More could be called at a moment's notice. Jadirel kept strong fighters on hand at all hours.

It was all for show. No one would use an army to take out an exile king. If Jadirel ever fell, it would be in a one on one challenge against one of his men. It was how he'd claimed his throne three years before.

Mad wished that random lieutenant luck.

He had no wish to rule.

The throne room was grand, with large windows swirling with that same colored glass. They looked out into the courtyard in the middle of the palace, and the air was sweet and perfumed.

Jadirel sat on his throne and spoke with two of his trusted advisors. On either side of his throne knelt a human, one man and one woman. Each wore a metal collar around their throats with thick chains that were tied to rings on the sides of the throne.

His human pets.

Kru'dari could take energy from a lot of aliens, and humans were some of the best. The brimmed with energy at all moments and barely noticed when it was gone, their bodies quickly making up for the deficit.

Jadirel didn't look like a tyrant. He would have been at home among the Krudare Senate back home. He'd been born into one of the old families, and his accent spoke of it. He was high born and educated, and loved to make others bleed.

No one knew why he'd been exiled. He'd been on the planet for a decade when Mad had arrived. And he'd slowly worked his way up to becoming an exile king.

Mad would never have chosen to work for

Jadirel, but now he didn't have a choice. He was determined to keep his head down and do what he needed to do to either earn his pardon or move to another territory.

At the moment, both options felt equally insurmountable.

Jadirel brimmed with power. He sucked it down from his humans without a care for their health. Humans had a lot to give, but even they had their limits. Jadirel was the only man Mad had heard of sucking a human dry of their energy.

The pets looked healthy enough for now. Mad's hands itched to unchain them, but he forced himself to look away. Trying would get him beaten or killed, and the humans might be punished, even though they were innocent of any scheming.

"Madn Damari!" Jadirel's voice boomed across the throne room, gregarious and welcoming. He waved him forward with a broad smile. "What news have you brought me?"

Mad bowed swiftly and rose again. Jadirel liked when the formalities were observed, but he hated too much deference. So far Mad walked the line, but he'd seen others beaten for not bowing long enough *and* for bowing too long.

"I simply come to report that the message has been delivered to Oron. He was on his way out of the territory when I last saw him." That was mostly true. The man had been facing towards the road that would lead him out of the territory. If he was smart, he was already gone. If he wasn't, Mad didn't want responsibility for him.

Jadirel nodded. "Always nice when a boy can see reason. Thank you for acting so swiftly."

Mad accepted the thanks with a nod. "Is there anything else I can do for you, sir?" He didn't want to be there a moment longer than he had to be. He was lucky to have caught his king in a good mood, and he didn't want it to shift.

"Yes," said the exile king.

Mad didn't wince, but he swore internally.

"I have not seen your friend Jaek in several weeks. Is he dead?" The question would have been callous on another planet, but people died fast and easy on Guerran.

"He was alive a few days ago when I last saw him." Jaek hated all of the exile kings equally. He lived on the edge of Jadirel's territory and was technically his subject, but he did his best to stay out of everything.

Jadirel didn't like that. And today he was tugging on the leash.

"Tell him to come see me," the king commanded. "I miss his captivating wit."

The advisors laughed, and Mad forced himself to smile. If Jaek wasn't careful, Jadirel would cut out his tongue.

They *both* needed to get off of Guerran.

"Of course, sir. I shall seek him out and give him your invitation. I suspect he's gone hunting in the out lands. He's likely to be back in his quarters by the turn of the moon. Would you like me to seek him out before then?" Mad held perfectly still and spoke in a tone he'd once reserved for his father. He didn't want to think of the similarities between his sire and Jadirel.

"Let him hunt. Just see that he reports in to pay his respects. That's all."

Mad bowed again and backed out of the room before Jadirel could change his mind. Then he turned and headed towards the edge of the territory where Jaek kept his quarters.

He had the feeling that Jadirel was up to something, and he had to warn his friend. He looked up at the sky and sent a prayer to the stars. He wanted his home.

But if the stars were listening, they didn't respond.

2

The ship landed roughly, and Kenzie Fletcher clutched the hard edge of her seat and sent up a prayer that she survived. She hadn't been to church in the better part of a decade, and even then she hadn't been paying attention. But the ship came to a stop with her still breathing, so maybe someone up there had her back.

She ran her tongue over the strange bumps on her palette. She'd been fitted with one of the best translators on the planet back when she was doing security on Earth Colony 3, but even after nearly seven years, it still felt a little strange when she remembered the implant was in her mouth.

There weren't many humans on this transport. She was a long way from home and the territories humans liked to prowl. But that didn't matter. She wasn't looking for an entire settlement of humans.

She only needed to find one.

She slung her bag over her shoulder and joined the crowd of people getting off the ship. Guerran was a weird place. It was a land full of criminals, but also welcomed newcomers from across the stars with few questions. It was the kind of place someone could get lost and make a new life for themselves... if they knew how to use a knife.

Kenzie's favorite dagger was in a sheath on her thigh. She had throwing knives on her belt and a baton in another sheath on her thigh, and her bag carried more weapons than clothes. Three planets back, one of her contacts had asked her why she didn't use a blaster, and Kenzie had shown her the scars on her left arm that came when a malfunctioning blaster nearly killed her back on EarthCol3.

There was no customs post on Guerran and no immigration check point. Kenzie hated to think of the things people could smuggle in, but the planet had been functioning like this for hundreds of years. It wasn't her place to question things.

She wasn't here to change society, just to find out if her sister had ended up on Guerran and when. She *had* to have been here. Kenzie didn't have any other leads.

A man wearing a wrinkled guard uniform beckoned her and the few other human passengers over. He wore a leather pouch around his neck that clashed with the black uniform. Strangely, the pouch almost seemed to glow.

Weird alien shit.

The guard had to be Kru'dari. They looked human, if humans were regularly nearly seven feet tall and brimming with muscle. And *power* emanated from him. She almost believed he could shoot fireballs out of his hand.

But Kenzie had studied the Kru'dari as best she could when she figured out she was going to Guerran. They didn't shoot fire or lightning. They were strong and violent, and could be possessive.

Barbarians.

The text hadn't used the word, but it had flashed before Kenzie's mind, and nothing else fit. They were a warrior people. On their home planet of Krudare, they might have pretended at civilization, but that was all forgotten on Guerran, where the strong ruled and the weak did what it took to survive.

Carise, I hope you're okay.

"We have control of the Green Zone," the guard was telling her and the four other humans from the ship. "It should be safe enough for all of you and the guards will assist you if you find yourself in danger. The exiles in this quadrant are closely monitored and *will* be punished if they do you any harm. But if you leave this area, your safety is no longer guaranteed. The criminals on this planet are in exile, not prison. We do not attempt to control them. And you will find some are especially motivated to take humans captive."

One of the humans shivered at the guard's tone and leaned against her companion. She had pale skin and red hair. Her companion put an arm around her and clutched her tight to him. Beside them there were two young women who still looked like teenagers. The taller one had light brown skin and straight, black hair, and had as many visible weapons as Kenzie, while the smaller, frailer one with dark brown skin and short curly hair reminded Kenzie of Carise. This girl had a protector.

Did her sister even know she was coming?

"Why do they want us?" the man with his arm around his companion asked.

The guard absently ran his hand over the pouch. "They will steal your vital energy. Humans brim with it more than other species."

"Vital energy?" the redhead asked.

"It's nothing you can control," the guard continued. "But it is something Kru'dari need to function on Guerran. We're..." He stroked his pouch again. "It doesn't matter. You simply must know that you'll be hunted by the worst of the worst outside of this safe area. Don't leave." He turned and abandoned them on the landing pad.

The two girls glared after the guard while the two adults followed in his footsteps after a minute, as if he could lead them to safety. For a moment Kenzie wondered if she should offer to help the girls. They were children and this was a dangerous place. But the taller girl stared at her, her eyes daring Kenzie to say something.

Even if they needed help, they wouldn't take it.

She gave the girl a warriors' nod and headed toward the large building she assumed was the launch terminal. She was starving, and there was sure to be some kind of food inside.

Meal eaten, she left the launch port and wandered around the Green Zone for a while. It looked like a military base. There were guards everywhere. She wasn't sure they outnumbered the regular people, but she wouldn't be surprised. Were they worried that the exiles would overrun them and chase them off the planet?

Not her problem.

The edge of the Green Zone was marked by a thick line in the road covered in green paint. Apparently the Kru'dari were a literal people. Kenzie didn't hesitate as she stepped over it. No guard tried to stop her.

The blocks outside the zone looked basically the same as those inside of it, except for the lack of guards. But as she walked further down the road, things began to fall into disrepair. The people looked well fed, though, and she saw people laughing and talking like they had no problems in the world.

Were they exiles?

Kenzie didn't waste time thinking about it. Obviously not everyone on the streets was an exile. She saw plenty of aliens who'd probably never set foot on Krudare. And none of them were who she was looking for.

She checked the note she'd written before boarding the transport to Guerran and then looked up at the stone building with a roaring lion carved above the door. It probably wasn't *actually* a lion. It was some cat from Kru'dari legend that resembled a lion back on Earth.

Whatever—it roared like a lion, it was a lion.

Inside the building was a restaurant, and she found an older Kru'dari woman who seemed to run the place. The woman was a head and a half taller than Kenzie and could probably bench press a horse. Kenzie had to stop herself from reaching for one of her weapons. Feeling small wasn't a reason to lash out.

"I'm here to talk to Layala," she said.

The woman nodded and pointed to a table in the back where a woman sat cloaked in shadow.

Showtime.

Kenzie was a little shocked to see Layala was human. Or, at least, she looked human. Plenty of alien species looked vaguely human or could shapeshift to impersonate them. Kenzie didn't ask if Layala was showing her true form.

It seemed rude.

Layala was maybe thirty with curly brown hair, beige skin, and a dark green bodysuit that clung to her curves and would have made Kenzie look twice if she swung that way.

Her blue eyes were cold.

She was a killer.

Kenzie didn't see weapons, but that meant nothing. Layala had chosen this spot. She knew this area. And if she wanted to end Kenzie, it wouldn't take any effort.

"I'm looking for my sister." Kenzie didn't have time to be afraid. Layala had agreed to meet, so Kenzie would assume she was acting in good faith until she proved otherwise.

"So I've heard." Layala waved at the Kru'dari

woman Kenzie had seen earlier. "Would you like tea?" Layala asked Kenzie.

There was a kind of rhythm to these meetings, no matter the planet, so Kenzie nodded. If she tried to rush Layala, she'd get nowhere.

"Two teas, Ifan. And we'll take some snacks. Thank you."

Ifan nodded and left them alone.

"Did you have any trouble finding this place?" Layala asked. "Were you followed?" She said it gently, but there was a threat laced in those words.

"No trouble at all. I was careful coming here, and I didn't see a tail. No one knows who I am, and if they followed me, it wasn't because I was meeting you." Ifan came back and placed the drinks and a plate of fruit, cheese, and bread with a red dipping sauce on the table. Kenzie nodded her thanks. She waited for Layala to grab the tea before reaching for her own and sipping.

Sweet. She drank more. It was good.

Layala grinned. "Did some do-gooder guard give you a warning about the scary exile territory? Were you told they eat us out here?"

Us. Layala was human.

Kenzie shrugged and reached for a slice of cheese. "What's this about vital energy?" she asked between bites. Her father would have slapped her for her bad manners. She took another bite to spite his memory.

"You know the legends of vampires from Earth?" Layala asked, like it wasn't a hugely popular myth.

Kenzie nodded. This deep into space there was no guarantee that a human was directly from Earth. There were settlements dotted across the stars, some of them made up of refugees who'd been abducted over the years, others made up of the descendants of space explorers. "Yes, I've heard of them. You're saying Kru'dari drink our blood and live forever?"

Nothing in the literature had suggested that.

But Layala waved a hand in dismissal. "Not quite. There might be bloodshed involved, but it's not necessary. Apparently back home they're all connected to this massive source of power that's generated by their planet. They can carry the power in these little leather packs, but they don't last for long. All the guards have them and they guard the shipments of those things better than they'd guard the king if he ever dared to appear here. But apparently fighting generates a power kind of similar to it, so the Kru'dari love to fight amongst themselves. Pit fights are a big form of entertainment. And humans are also brimming with energy. Luckily, most of the Kru'dari find it distasteful to feed off of unwilling humans. But some of them will hunt you down, put a chain around your neck, and drain you dry."

Kenzie didn't mean to, but her hand rose to her throat and felt the bare skin there. Was that what had happened to Carise? "How long does it take to drain a human?"

Layala shrugged. "If they're careful, taking energy won't kill someone. But if they insist on constantly feeding, day after day, and so on, never giving the human a chance to recover, the human will last a few months, a few years if they're very strong or regenerate their energy quickly." Layala reached down and pulled out a photograph that she placed on the table between them. Pictured was a Kru'dari man who kind of looked like a politician, middle aged, smiling, and slimy. "This is Jadirel. He's an exile king two territories east of here."

"Exile king?" Another thing not mentioned in the literature.

"The guards hate the term, so they don't tell you about it," Layala explained. "There are hundreds of territories in the city of Orion. Almost all of them are ruled by exile kings. There are a few that are ruled by egalitarian councils, but that's a whole other thing. Jadirel has a large territory, and he's known to keep humans for their energy. According to my sources, he purchased new humans three weeks ago. And here—" She pulled out another picture.

Carise.

Kenzie wanted to snap the picture up and hold it tight. Instead, she forced herself to keep still and look. The two years since her abduction had weighed heavy on Carise. There were dark circles and the beginnings of wrinkles under her eyes. Her hair was cropped short, as if whoever had kept her couldn't be bothered to deal with curly hair. Her brown skin was sallow and her face was as blank as an automaton's. Kenzie couldn't see her eyes, and she feared the spark of life had gone out of them.

Carise was a gentle woman. She wasn't hard like Kenzie. And the torture she had endured might have broken her.

But she was alive. And as long as she was alive, Kenzie could find her and get her the help she needed.

"This was taken outside of a known slave auction site. I couldn't confirm if your sister was sold to someone, but Jadirel was there that day. He's your best hope." Layala took both photos off the table, and Kenzie was left looking at the blank spot where her sister's image should have been.

"Any advice for approaching Jadirel?" Kenzie

asked. She ate more of the cheese. Food wasn't always plentiful, and she ate when she could.

"Don't." Layala's face grew serious. "He's powerful and cruel. Do some more investigation to see whether or not he even has Carise before you risk it." She stared at Kenzie for several seconds and sighed. "But since you're not going to do that... he respects power, as long as it doesn't directly challenge him. Don't show weakness."

Kenzie could have figured that out on her own.

Their business concluded, Layala took off. Kenzie took the bread and fruit, wrapped it in a napkin, and shoved it in her bag. Her credits were running low, and she wasn't about to let food go to waste.

Then she headed east. After twenty minutes of walking, a sign announced she was entering Jadirel's territory. How convenient.

If she'd thought the other territories were in disrepair, they had nothing on Jadirel's. There were no laughing people in the streets here. They kept their heads down and moved swiftly between buildings that looked like they might be blown over with one strong wind.

She hated him already, but she had to find him.

After a few more minutes of walking, she realized she was being followed. And a minute later she realized she wasn't just being followed, she was being *herded*. If only she had realized that before she'd turned into an alley that terminated in a dead end.

Kenzie turned around just in time to see three Kru'dari block off the entrance. The one in the middle leered. "I saw her first, boys, I have first claim."

Kenzie reached for her baton as the men charged.

3

MAD TRUDGED TO THE EDGE OF THE TERRITORY. THE CITY of Orion weaved in and out of the natural fixtures of Guerran, and there were places in the city that looked like wild wastelands. Walk across them, and a man was back in the city in less than an hour.

One of those wastelands bordered Jadirel's territory. In theory, it belonged to Jadirel, but not even the jealous exile king took time to patrol it closely. Every month or so, he rounded up strangers seeking asylum there and kicked them out or forced them into his territory, depending on his mood.

And for some reason, Jaek had decided it was a nice place to live.

This wilderness was dotted with hills and caves. A man could hide forever in the cave system, and more than a few exiles had unexpectedly met their end in there after getting lost.

Perhaps Jaek wanted to forget civilization all together and this was his best option. Mad had asked him once, a long time ago, but his friend had clammed up.

Mad hadn't tried to ask again.

He found the entrance to Jaek's cave, cleverly disguised by some vines. He brushed the vines aside and tested the hidden door. Locked. But Mad was keyed to Jaek's door, and he placed his palm on the sensor and waited a second until it unlocked.

Theoretically, all of the caves were connected, but Jaek was isolated by fallen rocks that blocked off access to the rest of the cave system and gave him a nice size room to call home.

It was dim, lit only by lights Jaek had installed that were on a motion sensor. It had been dark before Mad walked in.

"Are you home, Jaek? I come in peace!" Jaek had been on Guerran for so long that sometimes he surrendered to the urge to fight, and nothing could stop him from attacking. Mad had long ago learned that announcing his presence, even when he thought the room was empty, was safer than walking around silently.

Jaek didn't answer back. But there was evidence

he'd been home recently. He had a bed in the corner and the blankets were rumpled. There was also a blanket thrown haphazardly along the back of his couch. Some dust had settled on the table, but it had been disturbed, as if Jaek had wiped his fingers across it and made phantom claw marks.

He wasn't much for dusting.

And he wasn't here.

Though Mad wanted to see his friend, he was a bit relieved. He could answer Jadirel honestly that he'd sought Jaek out. It wasn't his fault he wasn't home.

Mad found a piece of paper and scratched out a note. *J is looking for you. Getting insistent.*

He couldn't write out anything more. There was always a chance that one of Jadirel's spies had followed him here and would search the cave for any sign that Mad or Jaek weren't as loyal as they should be. But Jaek would get the note. The man wasn't stupid. He knew a warning when he read one.

Rather than head out, Mad sank back onto Jaek's couch. "What the...?"

It was actually... comfortable? Mad had sat on that couch a hundred times, and the cushions had been a mere suggestion against the wooden frame. But today the cushions felt stuffed as full as they could be. Mad turned over and examined one. It appeared as if the seams of the cushion had been ripped out and resewn, and a bit of stuffing was caught in the thread.

Mad's complaining must have finally gotten to Jaek.

He sat back down and decided to enjoy it. Then he took the flyer out of his pocket and studied it harder. This fugitive could be his ticket off of Guerran. Who was the young man? He was younger than Mad. Softer, too. This wasn't a soldier he was looking at.

But looks could be deceiving. The children who were exiled to Guerran often looked sweet, but they had the same killer instinct as the rest of the survivors on the planet.

The flyer didn't have any more information. No name. No list of crimes. No known associates. Mad memorized the face and was determined to keep an eye out for the man. He'd think about how he'd catch him later.

The walk home was uneventful, and as soon as Mad walked in the door, he saw his communication screen beeping with a call request.

Only one person in the galaxy tried to call him. Mad accepted the call request and bounced on his feet, waiting for the connection to go through. He smiled broadly when his sister appeared, a three-year-old boy on her shoulder.

Derok's face lit up with a grin and he waved his pudgy little hand wildly. "Uncle Madn!"

Taiana's smile wasn't as big, but it was still there. He'd worry when she didn't smile at all. "I was worried you'd miss my call."

"I'm glad I didn't." The calls were expensive and the tech sometimes spotty. But Mad would spend all the credits he had to check in on his sister and nephew.

"How are you doing?" she asked, shifting Derok around until he was sitting completely on her lap. The boy picked up a toy after a moment and started playing with it, ignoring the screen.

It made Mad's heart light to see him. He'd never held the child. Unless he was pardoned, he never would.

The flyer burned a hole in his pocket. He needed to find a way home.

"I'm alright." He did his best to keep the worst of it from Taiana. She didn't need to waste her time worrying about him when there was little she could do. Her calls and infrequent care packages were more than he could hope for.

"I read an article about conditions on Guerran. Is

it true? A star storm killed thirty people?" She was aghast.

Mad shrugged. A star storm was the least of his worries. "I don't know. I haven't heard about that."

"I—" She looked away from the screen for a moment and made a face. Then she looked back at Mad. "I'll be right back. Derok's tutor needs to speak with us. Keep the call open. I promise I'll be right back."

"I'll be here." He stared at her empty chair and tried not to look further into the home she shared with her husband. He didn't need the reminders of all the comforts of Krudare.

Then Arbyn slid into the chair, and it took all of Mad's control not to scowl. He and his brother-in-law didn't speak. The only credit Mad would give the man was that he'd purchased a state of the art communication system so that Mad and Taiana could speak to one another.

"You look well, Madn," Arbyn greeted with his political smile.

"Hello." Mad couldn't disconnect the call with the promise of Taiana and Derok coming back. But he wanted to. Or he wanted to invent a technology that would allow him to slap that smile off of Arbyn's face.

Arbyn looked away from the screen, craning his

neck as if checking something in his house. Then he turned back to Mad, smile gone. "The moment we disconnect this session, Taiana is going to adjourn to her room and cry for the rest of the day. Derok will ask me why he can't meet his favorite uncle. And I will be left here to piece my family back together."

It was a stab in the heart. Mad didn't have a response. He lived for these calls. He'd go insane without them. But the thought that he was hurting his sister made him die inside. "Speak clearly. You know I don't play your games."

Arbyn scowled, but the expression was gone as quickly as it came. "Perhaps if you did, you wouldn't be in this predicament."

"So I should have allowed a slaughter?" It came out a snarl, and Mad could picture the dead bodies littered on the ground, people he couldn't save.

"It's a soldier's duty to follow orders."

"You've never been a soldier. Don't tell me my duty." He could reach forward and end the call with a press of a button. But Taiana would be back soon.

"You are impossible." Arbyn took a deep breath and re-centered himself. "You are a risk to this family. Derok will begin to attend school soon. What do you think will happen when your name comes up?"

Mad stayed silent. When he thought about it, it kept him up at night. But the horrors of Guerran were enough that he could normally ignore the troubles back home.

"I've found a way to get you off Guerran." It was barely more than a whisper, as if Arbyn feared being overheard.

"A pardon?" Mad sat up straighter. If Arbyn could manage that, Mad would forget every bad thing he'd ever thought about the man.

Arbyn scoffed. "You think highly of yourself. The king handed out twelve pardons last year. Don't be stupid. There's a ship captain that owes me a favor. He'll be in orbit for the next month. I've relayed his information to you. Put out that call and he'll pluck you from Guerran and give you a job. I can funnel enough credits to you so you'll have a month's wages. This captain knows of another planet where exiles make their home. It has an energy signature similar to Krudare. It's not the Fount, but it's better than Guerran."

"You bastard." Mad's hands curled into fists, and it took all of his discipline not to punch the video display. "If I leave Guerran, I'll be excised from the family completely. I'll never be able to return to Krudare."

"I'm trying to help you, you thick-skulled idiot.

You harm this family just by existing. Leave Guerran. Make a life for yourself. And leave us alone."

"Does Taiana know about this?" If she did, if she approved, Mad would go. For her.

But Arbyn's face gave it away. "I love my wife. I won't ask her to make this choice. Make the break easier for her. Derok's still young. He may forget you ever existed. It's for the best."

"I'm not leaving." Not while there was *any* hope he might be reunited with his family one day.

"If you're not on that ship by the end of the month, I personally guarantee you will *never* be pardoned." His face shifted, and suddenly there was a bright smile as he rose from his chair. "My darling, is all well with the tutor?"

Taiana sat with a roll of her eyes. "A simple misunderstanding. I'm not sure why she was so urgent. She seemed to think *I* wanted to talk to her. Never mind. Thanks for entertaining Mad. Derok wanted to show you his new project. He's waiting in your office."

Arbyn bent down and kissed Taiana before giving Mad a brief nod and walking away.

"Did you find something to talk about?" Taiana asked. "Or did he make you sit quietly and wait for me to return?"

She couldn't know. If she believed Mad, her

heart would break. And if she thought he was lying...
Mad couldn't risk it.

"You know me and Arbyn. We always manage to say something."

Taiana laughed. "I wish you could come home. I think you'd like him better these days. He's half-civilized."

Mad faked a smile. "I wish I was there."

4

Kenzie's baton was covered in blood and her side was bruised. None of the Kru'dari had gotten close enough to take her out, but it had been a near thing. She felt so damn *small* here.

Why did these assholes need to be seven feet tall?

Hands clapped behind her, a mocking, singular beat of two palms slapping together. She turned and saw five more Kru'dari blocking the path. These men were different than the wannabes who'd cornered her. They wore dark uniforms that looked to be made of leather, and carried well-crafted weapons.

Soldiers of the exile king. She was sure of it.

Kenzie rolled her wrist, making a big circle with the baton. Taking out the wannabes had been harder than she expected. She didn't think she could win against trained soldiers.

When in doubt, fake it. She wiped the blood off her baton and gave the men a flourishing bow. "Thank you. I do love it when a performance is appreciated."

The head soldier stopped clapping. "You're new here."

"Fresh off the boat." She couldn't look away from him. He and his men effectively blocked off her only escape route unless she could find a way to scale the buildings behind her. They weren't that tall, but she was still only human.

"Boat?" the man asked.

Not all idioms translated. Kenzie forgot that sometimes. "My name is Kenzie Fletcher. These men cornered me and I defended myself."

The leader put a hand on his chest. "I am Tyze. You are in my king's territory. He loves to meet his people. Will you accept his invitation?"

Invitation? Ha! Like Kenzie had a choice. Her only choice was whether she'd walk there on her own two feet or if Tyze would drag her in chains.

"I was told this is King Jadirel's territory."

Tyze nodded in confirmation. "We are not far from his palace."

Jadirel was her only lead on Carise. This wasn't

the optimal way to meet the man. Kenzie had the sinking suspicion she was about to end up in one of his cells. But her back was very literally to a wall.

She wasn't dead yet. This was her chance to find Carise. She hadn't had a lead this hot in over a year.

"I would be honored to accept his invitation."

Tyze's men swarmed around her, crowding close enough so she couldn't try to run away. She kept any snarky comments to herself. She didn't want more bruises if she could avoid them.

"Please give your baton and that knife to Gav," Tyze instructed, pointing to the obvious weapons on her belt.

Kenzie did it without complaint. But she didn't offer up any of her less conspicuous weapons. Tyze didn't have anyone pat her down, and that was his mistake. One she wasn't about to offer to correct.

The soldiers led her to the palace and walked her in though the ornate doors and down a dim hall with a high ceilings and complicated carvings on the walls. The hall led to a throne room, and the king himself was sprawled on his throne.

Two humans were chained on either side of him, and Kenzie wanted to reach for one of her throwing knives and end this now.

The bastard would die.

The desperate need for freedom flowed deep in

her veins, going back to ancestors who'd prayed for it for centuries. This wasn't an injustice she could walk away from.

But it also wasn't a problem she could solve right then. If she killed Jadirel, his people would kill her right back. And Carise would lose her last hope of being saved.

Jadirel wasn't what she expected. He was in his forties or fifties, assuming Kru'dari aged like humans, and on the short side for his people, topping out at around six foot five.

He reminded her a bit of her commanding officer back on EarthCol3. Happy to be in charge and desperate to stay that way. This wasn't a man who'd share a lick of power.

That was fine. Kenzie didn't want power. Just her sister. And freedom for his people.

Was that so much to ask?

Jadirel sat up straighter on his throne, his smile almost kind. It didn't reach his eyes. "Tyze, what have you brought me?"

Tyze bowed swiftly. "A warrior, sir. Baryn and his men cornered her, and she left them a crying heap on the ground."

Jadirel looked at her more closely. He stood up and crossed the room to her, circling around her like a shark. "Interesting. You're human, yes?"

No use denying it. "Yes," Kenzie confirmed.

"And new here."

"Yes."

"Hmm." He didn't touch her. Thankfully. Kenzie was good at hiding her emotions, but when people got too close, she sometimes snapped. She vibrated with tension. Her sister was possibly in the same building, and she had to get information.

"Not many humans come freely to Guerran." Jadirel backed up a bit, and Kenzie let out a breath.

He was lying. She'd seen several humans on the street. But contradicting the king would do her no good. "I'm looking for my sister. I have reason to believe she was brought to Guerran. Not freely."

"Hmm." He looked her up and down, and Kenzie hated the attention. She walked a thin line. This man kept humans as pets. If she wasn't careful, he might try to clap her in chains. "Tell me about her."

Her arm tingled, a reminder that she always carried a bit of her sister with her, but she kept her sleeves covered. She had a garotte hidden in her bracelet and she didn't want to call attention to it. "She looks like me, though she has a scar on her left cheek and she has curly hair. Her name is Carise and she was abducted from Earth about two interstellar common years ago. I've been searching for her ever since."

"You've come a long way." Jadirel was getting closer.

Shit. She really didn't want him noticing her. But it was far too late now.

"Do you like my toys?" He nodded to his chained humans. Neither of the people responded. Their eyes were blank, and Kenzie hoped both of them had found some mental way to cope with their surroundings.

She kept quiet. If she opened her mouth, she'd only make things worse.

"The boy is getting weak." He waved a hand toward the chained male, and the boy moaned and fell to his side. Jadirel sighed in pleasure and seemed to get taller. Somehow. "But his energy is so delicious. I wonder what you'd taste like." He leaned forward.

Kenzie had a hand on her knife before she could think better of it, and in a blink, her blade was against the skin of Jadirel's throat. But rather than react in fear, the bastard laughed.

He clamped his hand on her wrist and squeezed, but she held her knife where it was, even as it felt like he'd grind her bones to dust.

"Stay back," he warned his men. "This feisty little bird is my treat."

She tried to dig the knife in, but his grip was too strong.

"I don't have your sister, little bird. But if she's as delectable as you, I'll bring her straight to my bed." He twisted, and she found herself holding her knife to her own throat. It took all of her strength to keep from digging in and killing herself.

Jadirel nipped at her ear, tugging on the cartilage until it hurt. And then he shoved her to the ground and kicked her in the stomach.

Kenzie grunted. There was blood on her neck, and her ribs might have been bruised. She wasn't sure.

But she got to her feet.

Jadirel tipped his head back and laughed again. "I haven't seen a person as brave as you in an age. I want to see you in the pit. Win the night, and you'll walk away free."

The pit. That sounded *great*. Just what Kenzie needed when she was already bleeding.

Just survive until tomorrow, she told herself. *One day at a time.*

5

MAD HATED THE PIT, BUT HE COULDN'T STOP HIMSELF from going every week. Sometimes he fought, other nights he stood at the edge and observed the carnage. Pit fights were a huge source of income for Jadirel's territory. Exiles and residents from half the city came to watch blood sport.

And the betting was enough to fund a small country. Or a large territory.

But Mad wasn't betting tonight. The call with Arbyn had him angry enough that he wanted to dive into the pit himself and burn off the hate until he felt like himself again. He didn't, though. He'd lost his last fight, and he didn't think his pride could take another beating.

Not tonight.

He heard Tyze's braying laughter and edged

away. Jadirel came to all the fights and often switched up matches at the last moment, especially when he was angry and wanted to punish a fighter. Or throw one of his subjects into the pit.

Mad didn't move fast enough. Tyze spotted him and waved him over. Ignoring it might anger the man, and the risk wasn't worth it. Jadirel wasn't upset with him right now, so Mad would be on his best behavior.

"If you move quick, you can pay your respects before the rush," Tyze told him, nodding up the stairs to where Jadirel sat in a private box.

Mad didn't remind the man he'd paid his respects earlier in the day. Instead, he trudged up the stairs. Jadirel looked positively giddy. "Mad! Take a seat. I didn't expect to see you here."

Mad sat. What choice did he have? "I came to watch the fights."

"Of course, of course. This next one will be worth the cost of admission. I hope. Or it will be over before it begins. A pity, really." He spoke fast, one word tripping over the next, and Mad wondered if he'd taken some kind of stimulant. Drugs were easy to come by on Guerran, and Jadirel was known to dabble.

"Who's fighting?" Despite himself, he was intrigued.

"Some newcomer human who thinks she's tough. She pulled a knife on me in my own throne room!" He laughed. "It takes guts. I probably should have killed her." He shrugged. "I want to see her fight. Tyze says she took down Baryn and his crew. I thought I'd give Baryn a chance for revenge. It'll be a shame to watch her die. But if she survives... oh, the fucking she'll give me." He leered down at the pit.

Mad looked away to keep from scowling. Any camaraderie he might have felt dissolved in an instant.

His eyes snagged on the human and he froze. The good thing about Jadirel's box was that they were right at the edge of the pit and could see better than at any place in the crowd. He was only a dozen or so feet away from the human, and he got a good look at her.

There was *something* about her that made him want to call her to him, to stand in front of her and shield her from harm. She radiated confidence, her hand gripping a long knife and a relaxed look on her face. But she didn't belong in the pit.

She belonged in his bed.

The certainty of it slammed into him, and Mad almost rocked back in his chair. Now he was thinking like Jadirel, and he was disgusted with himself. He had no right to her, no matter how much his blood sang with want.

Her dark hair was pulled back in a tight braid, though it was frizzy around the edges of her face. Her skin was light brown, and even from several feet away, he could see the freckles that dotted her cheeks. And her eyes... he shouldn't have been able to see the green of her eyes, but they stabbed into him.

What would she look like while she was riding his cock?

He had to get himself under control. Attraction like this, desperate need, had never slammed into him before. Sure, he'd admired plenty of women. But none had ever tempted him to jump into the pit and steal them away before they could come to harm.

He watched the way she held her knife and had to admire it. She was sure of herself, her grip steady and her feet light. Compared to him, she was tiny, a short little human he could pick up and swing around like she was nothing. But judging by the way she held the knife, she'd never let him get away with it.

Still, he wanted to try.

She was muscular under her tight clothes, the swell of her breasts and hips a suggestion under leathers rather than a temptation. Would she let him unwrap her and discover the secrets of her flesh?

Was this how Jadirel felt?

Cold disgust washed over him, and Mad forced his gaze to Baryn, who was leaning against the cage surrounding the pit and tossing a bat from hand to hand, a smug smile on his face.

He was ready for revenge.

"What's her name?" Mad asked. He shouldn't show interest. Jadirel would hurt her just to show him who was boss. But Mad had to know.

"Kenzie. How do you think the fight will go?" He must not have heard the desire in Mad's voice. Or maybe this time he didn't care.

Mad swallowed and looked back. Kenzie tested the sand of the pit, letting it run through her fingers. Then she looked up and around at the crowd she was fighting for. She looked straight at him, and their eyes locked for a moment.

Then she looked away.

Mad tried not to feel the loss.

Baryn was still leaning against the wall and grinning. He stared at Kenzie like she was a rat that needed to be taught a lesson.

"The human will win," Mad said. She *had* to win. Baryn didn't like to let his opponents leave the pit alive. "But I doubt she'll kill Baryn unless she has to."

"Hmm." Jadirel leaned forward and studied the pit. "Care to wager on that?"

"You know I play safe with my credits." He didn't want to bet, especially not against Jadirel. The exile king would honor a victory, but he'd be sure to wager something Mad couldn't afford to lose.

"You're not any fun." But Jadirel let the matter drop.

Mad wanted to leave, but he hadn't been dismissed. After a while, Jadirel seemed to have forgotten all about him and Mad might have gotten away with sneaking off. But then the match began, and Mad forgot all about leaving.

The only better seat in the house was *in* the pit, and Mad wanted to watch the fight.

All of Baryn's smug confidence transformed into focus the moment the gong sounded and the fight began. He burst from his spot and came at Kenzie in a whirl of speed, his bat flying at her almost too fast to see.

She rolled out of the way and Baryn missed her by an inch. The crowd gasped. This fight was going to go longer than anyone expected.

The odds were long on Kenzie, and Mad almost wished he'd taken the bet. But thoughts of credits dissolved as he leaned forward and got lost in the spectacle before him.

Kenzie drew first blood, her knife kissing Baryn's forearm and cutting through the leather. The man roared in pain and swung his bat wildly.

Kenzie cut him again.

She wasn't afraid to get close. Baryn liked using his bat, and Mad had felt the brunt of it during his time in the pit, but the bat wasn't much use when an opponent was inches from you.

Despite being a foot shorter than him and far less muscular, Kenzie wasn't afraid to stay in his space and ruthlessly cut at him. She couldn't get in any shots powerful enough to end him, but eventually he'd tire.

Did Baryn know the danger he was in?

The Kru'dari finally switched tactics and pulled his bat in and thrust it out like a spear, sending Kenzie flying backward.

Mad was up and out of his seat, eyes tracking her wildly. This couldn't be the end. She couldn't die like this. He put his hand on the axe he carried on his back, ready to pull it out and join the fight.

But Jadirel was right next to him, and diving into the pit would be suicide.

He forced himself to sit back down.

Baryn swung his bat carelessly as he moved in to

finish the human off, but it made him slow, and Kenzie scrambled to her feet before he could do more damage. She said something that Mad couldn't hear, and Baryn screamed and charged.

Kenzie laughed.

The sound rang out through the arena and went straight to his cock.

She was a warrior, and he wanted to feel her under him, over him, around him. He just wanted *her*.

But he needed her to survive this fight.

Baryn got close and Kenzie rolled again, coming up behind him. She hooked a leg on his side and clamped on his back, her knife pressed hard against his throat. It would take no effort on her part to end it. Instead, she whispered something into Baryn's ear.

Baryn was frozen. If he threw her off, he risked having his throat cut. He was stronger, but she had the superior position. They stood like that for several seconds until Baryn cast his bat to the ground, holding his hands up high and clasping them together in a sign of surrender.

The gong ending the match sounded, and Kenzie let him go.

Jadirel leaned back in his chair, an assessing look on his face. "She shows weakness."

Mad kept silent. Mercy wasn't a weakness. And if Jadirel didn't see the skill it took *not* to kill Baryn, he was a fool.

"You enjoyed the fight," Jadirel continued. "Go and greet her. I'll have my taste of her soon enough. Don't let her get away."

Jadirel wanted to keep her. Maybe not as one of his pets, but as someone he owned. Mad needed to warn her. He couldn't escape Jadirel's control, but he wouldn't stoop to handing innocents over.

He hurried down to the pit. He needed to meet the human.

6

THE PIT WASN'T THE WORST PLACE SHE'D EVER FOUGHT, especially when a med tech came over and injected her with something that made the pain in her ribs fade to nothingness before slathering a cream over her and telling her she'd be fine by morning. Whatever was in the cream made her skin tingle, but the injection didn't make her loopy, so Kenzie was calling that a win.

Her heart still raced and she was giddy from the fight. She'd known she would win. A person couldn't walk into a potential death match with anything *but* the utmost confidence in victory. Even better, she hadn't needed to kill anyone. Kenzie knew how to use her blade to end a life, but she'd seen enough death. She didn't want to deal it. Not even to an asshole who'd attacked her earlier that day.

But even with the giddiness still riding high, she knew she had to find a way out of the fighters' quarters. Already some of the pit fighters were eyeing her as a potential threat and she didn't want to deal with that. She wasn't sure how challenges were supposed to work and she didn't want to find out.

And Jadirel was likely to come looking for her. Or rather, he'd send a flunky.

She could fight off flunkies, but it was always safer to flee than fight.

And what about Carise? Kenzie had spent the entire time since leaving Jadirel's palace wondering if the exile king had lied about purchasing her sister. At the time, he'd seemed taunting and truthful. But he kept humans in bondage.

She had to find a way into his palace and check. And if she could find a way to free all those he'd enslaved, all the better. They deserved to be free, and he deserved payback for throwing her into the pit.

Kenzie needed to get out of there and find a place to rest for now. Nights weren't long on Guerran, but she was tired. She ducked out of the fighters' quarters and into the hallway that led to the arena and the exit. There was a distant roar of the crowd, cheering on another fight, and the hallway was deserted.

Except for one Kru'dari coming her way.

Kenzie couldn't move. She stared at him and her body was on fire. It was the adrenaline from the fight and the avalanche of anxiety from the last few days that rooted her in place.

He was the most gorgeous man she'd ever seen.

It didn't even matter that he *wasn't* a man. Those sorts of technicalities faded away the further a human got away from Earth.

He was nearly seven feet tall, with muscles rippling under his leather and furs. He dressed like the exiled warriors who roamed the streets, ready to fight at a moment's notice. There was a scary looking axe strapped to his back.

She wasn't sure she could beat him if he dragged her into the pit.

But his expression was kind.

As he got closer, she caught sight of gray eyes and wanted to lose herself in them. His nose had a hump in it, like it had been broken at least once. And there was a scar through one eyebrow.

He kept his hair cropped short on the sides, but it was longer on the top and swooped to the right, drawing even more attention to that eyebrow scar, pointing like an arrow.

And when he spotted her, his face blossomed into a smile, and Kenzie's heart threatened to explode.

One word, and she'd follow wherever he led. After years of traipsing across the galaxy, it was like looking at her home. One she hadn't known she'd been searching for. She wanted to wrap her arms around him and let go, let him take the load and beg for his help.

Fuck. She was going crazy.

She'd heard of planets where aliens exuded hormones that could make a woman lose her mind. But not here. Not on Guerran.

Clearly it had been too long since she'd taken anyone to bed. Could she take him?

Between her thighs? Certainly. On the battle-field? Not without a lot of planning.

He closed the distance between them and stood close. Too close. She could smell his scent, mascu-line and leathery, with a hint of soap. This was a warrior who knew how to keep clean. That was always a plus.

She wanted to reach out and touch him. She wanted to grab the leather strap crossing his chest and use it to drag him into a private corner and have her way with him.

God, it would be fun.

She wanted to kiss him almost more than her next breath.

Kenzie didn't know what had come over her, and she couldn't fight it. Not when he was looking at her like she was something precious.

"I saw your fight," he said, voice nice and low, perfect for filthy promises. "Baryn is lucky."

He'd noticed that. Perhaps Kenzie should have been worried. Instead, she smiled. "That's twice today I've kicked his ass." Bragging? Sure. But she'd earned it.

The man laughed. "He'll want payback."

"He knows if he comes at me a third time, I'll end him." That had been her promise while she held her knife to his throat and his life in her hands. Whether he'd keep away from her remained to be seen.

"I'm Mad."

A name, not the emotion. "Kenzie." He had to already know, as it had been announced before the fight.

"Kenzie." He tasted her name and it was sweet on his lips. She wanted him whispering it to her in private.

"I need to get out of here." She wasn't about to look a gift warrior in the mouth. Mad didn't seem eager to drag her to Jadirel, and he could get her past the guards that were bound to be posted at the exit.

As for what she'd do with him after that? Well, she'd figure it out later.

He took her hand and it dwarfed hers, but instead of a threat, it made Kenzie feel safe. She followed him down the hall and watched as he had a private word with the two huge Kru'dari guarding the exit.

Getting past them on her own would have been... difficult.

They let her and Mad pass, and then they were free in the warm night air. They'd walked a bit before Mad came to a stop, the roars from the pit barely audible at this distance. "King Jadirel is going to be searching for you," he warned.

"Not surprising." She'd met petty kings and rulers just like him, and she'd survived every one. She wasn't scared of Jadirel. She'd lost the ability to be scared of anything except failing to find Carise or learning her sister was dead. "Are you planning to take me to him?"

"The thought of you in his bed enrages me. I'd tear down his palace to stop it."

They'd exchanged a handful of words. Kenzie

couldn't trust Mad. It would be beyond irresponsible to do anything except walk away right that moment. Instead, she tugged on his arm until he moved closer.

"Why? Do you want to take me yourself?"

7

Kenzie's energy swirled around her, strong enough for any Kru'dari to be tempted. Mad wanted to back her up against the nearest wall and take her for himself. He'd do it with or without her energy.

But they were on the street and anyone could come by. It wasn't safe to be out in Jadirel's territory at night.

Do you want to take me yourself?

The words echoed in his head. He still had Kenzie's hand in his. His quarters were only a minute away. He could take her to his bed and keep her there for as long as she would stay.

Forever, if he had any say in the matter.

What he was feeling was crazy. He wasn't the kind of man to try and claim a woman the moment she laid eyes on him. But he wanted Kenzie for his own. If he were a better man, he'd let her walk away. He'd tell her to stay safe, or perhaps walk her to her quarters to watch her back, and then he'd let her go.

But there was desire in her eyes. She didn't ask the question idly.

She wanted him too.

If he left her alone, Jadirel's men could find her. He might have saved her from the king for now, but if Jadirel remembered her, he'd send Tyze or one of his other flunkies to find her. She could handle herself in a fight, but Tyze didn't play fair.

It sounded noble. It was bullshit.

"I live right over there." Mad pointed to his building. "Want to come home with me?"

Kenzie swallowed, the muscles in her throat a temptation he wanted to taste. Her lips curved up into a smile. "Lead the way."

He'd never walked a longer distance in his life as he passed the four buildings between where they stood and the entrance to his quarters. He was glad he kept the place neat; he didn't need Kenzie to judge him for a dirty house.

He closed the door behind them and locked it. Moonlight streamed in through the large window, giving the place an ethereal feel. They'd walked into a magical space. At least for the night.

Kenzie stepped close. He could smell a hint of

sweat and the biting scent of the soap from the showers the pit fighters used to clean up. Her eyes danced with danger and lust, her gaze darting between his eyes and his lips.

"Are you doing something to me?" she asked, a hint of vulnerability in her words.

"Are *you* doing something to me?" There were legends of aliens who came from across the stars to tempt innocent Kru'dari into sin and mischief. But Mad was no innocent.

Promise hung between them until they couldn't take it anymore. Mad didn't know who lunged forward, and it didn't matter. Kenzie's lips were on his, her taste exploding on his mouth. He had to hunch over a bit to make it work, and her body was straining for an additional inch to meet him.

Screw that.

He hefted her up and her legs came around his waist. She was a little heavier than he expected, her sleek muscles giving her unexpected bulk. It didn't matter. His muscles barely strained.

She wrapped her arms around his shoulders and kept on kissing him, even as he backed her up until she was against the wall, trapped there by the hot press of his body. She didn't seem to mind.

And Mad was crazy with want. His cock was an iron rod in his trousers, desperate for the hot, wet sheath of Kenzie's cunt. He wanted inside of her so badly he was tempted to rip her clothes to shreds and take her right there.

But he was a barbarian, not a brute.

Kenzie kissed him with a desperation that came with long suppressed lust and uncertainty of when she'd get this again. Mad unleashed everything he had on her and then gave her even more. She never had to want again. He'd do everything he could to keep her satisfied.

She was going to be his.

The need to claim roared inside of him. He was forgetting something important, but nothing was more important that kissing Kenzie. The King of Krudare could hand him a pardon and he'd ignore it, so long as he got to keep Kenzie.

Kenzie pulled against the strap of his leathers and he had a feeling that if she could reach for her knives, she'd cut him out of his gear. A *slight* hint of sanity returned. He undid the straps and let the leathers fall to the floor, his axe hitting hard and loud. That left his top covered with only a thin shirt that Kenzie ripped at, tearing a little at the V of the neck.

Mad plucked it off and tossed it somewhere behind them before she could do more damage to his wardrobe. Kenzie wasted no time taking off her own clothes. And in a blink, she was naked before him.

Mad drank her in, the swell of her breasts, the curve of her hips and stomach, the way tight muscle lay over it all with too many scars that told a story of violence and death. He wanted to keep her safe. He wanted to hunt down every bastard who had marked her and make them pay.

But mostly he wanted her. And he was done holding back.

He took the rest of his clothes off in swift, economical movements. He could have torn the fabric to shreds, but he didn't want to send his little human running scared. But judging by the way her eyes raked over him, she wanted the danger that lived within him.

He closed the distance between them and placed his hand on the curve of her neck. He could almost wrap his fingers all the way around her throat, and her pulse fluttered against his palm. He squeezed, just enough to show her he could.

Her pulse beat even faster. And there wasn't a hint of fear in her gaze.

He'd seen a mate mark on an exile woman's neck before. Her mate had wanted all of Guerran to know she was taken. At the time, Mad hadn't understood. But now, energy sizzled within him, and the urge to claim in that way that couldn't be taken back rode him.

Lust made him dizzy, but no matter how strong it was, he wouldn't go that far.

Not tonight.

He reached for Kenzie and kissed her again. She poured her soul into it, like this was her last night of freedom. She was wrong. There was no freedom on Guerran, not for anyone. And she was completely at his mercy. She'd stepped far away from her knives, and he was bigger.

But he knew what she was capable of. He'd seen her in the pit. And that only made his cock harder.

He dipped his fingers into her cunt and found her dripping. He wanted to feast on her until she came apart under his tongue. But his cock was insistent. And she was wet.

They had all night. He was determined to keep her here for as long as he could. Forever, if he could find a way.

There'd be time for everything. Later.

But now he needed her too much to hold back. And Kenzie clutched him hard and thrust her hips against him. "Fuck me," she demanded against his lips.

Yes. He didn't give a shit about his bed, not when he already had her in his arms. He pinned her against the wall, and his cock found her entrance, wet and ready for him. He thrust inside, groaning out his pleasure as she gasped at the intrusion.

Her body tensed, and Mad forced himself to still, even as her cunt gripped him in its tight, wet torture. He needed to move. He'd go crazy if he didn't. But he wouldn't move an inch until Kenzie was ready for more. She wasn't some body he was slaking his lust on. She was everything and more.

"More," she demanded, the words rough in his ear.

Some long forgotten gentlemanly instinct told him to take this slow, to move her to the bed and give her the lovemaking a lady deserved.

But he wasn't a gentleman any longer, and Kenzie whispered filthy demands in his ear, fingers clutching at him and urging him on.

He unleashed himself, plunging into her and pinning her in place against the wall. He met her every demand with enthusiasm and gave her even more. His body burned from holding her up, and he was a live wire with pleasure.

He kept going.

Kenzie begged for more.

Lust was a tornado around them, twisting and turning and threatening to destroy everything. Mad let himself be taken by it. He couldn't remember the last time he'd felt free to unleash himself like this, and he wanted more.

Kenzie's energy burned under her skin, seeking release. Mad drank it up, and even more took its place. No matter how much he took, she replenished it. She was like his own personal Fount, and before long, he brimmed with more energy than he'd had in six years.

He wanted to take more, but Kenzie was clutching him even tighter, riding his cock as her body rippled around his, her head falling back as she cried out in pleasure and came.

Mad followed her off the cliff, emptying himself inside of her as white hot pleasure exploded behind his eyes.

They made it to the bed at some point. And he tasted her until she cried out his name and came again.

Eventually they succumbed to sleep, though Mad vowed to himself it would only be for a short while. He didn't know how long he slept, but he felt the bed dip, and when he opened his eyes, light fluttered in through the window.

And Kenzie knelt beside him, naked and glorious, her hand gripping a knife she held to his throat. "You're going to tell me everything you know."

8

KENZIE HAD TO BE GOING OUT OF HER FUCKING MIND. SHE kept her hand steady and tried to ignore the smell of sex that lay heavy in the room. She had to ignore the way her muscles ached and the memory of Mad's body on her.

In her.

She didn't fuck for information. Her body was a tool, but she used violence most often. Once or twice, she might have let a prospective lead *think* she'd invite him to her bed. But she'd never done more than flirt.

Until Mad said two sentences to her and dragged her home to fuck her against the wall.

It had to be something about this planet. Or maybe it was some Kru'dari trick. None of the information she'd read about his species or his planet suggested wild sex pheromones, but free guide-books were notoriously stingy with information. But if there *were* crazy Kru'dari sex pheromones, then why hadn't she been panting after anyone else?

The only person she had eyes for was Mad.

But she was supposed to be looking for Carise.

Her hand didn't waver, even as all the thoughts washed over her. Mad looked at her steadily, his naked body barely covered by the sheet. If he moved, she'd have to kill him. He was bigger than her and a skilled fighter. It was obvious in the way he held himself.

He wasn't like the man she'd defeated the day before. Mad wouldn't play games. He'd fight to win.

And he had to see the threat in her eyes. Another man would have moved by now, would have tried to get away.

She saw a trickle of blood under her blade and had to force herself to keep her hand where it was. Why did she care if he bled? He was a source. Last night meant nothing.

It couldn't mean anything.

She pushed away the emotions that tried to crush her. She'd had plenty of experience at *that* over the last few years. If she let herself focus on the pain of losing Carise, she'd go crazy. Instead, all she could focus on was the mission.

Mad wasn't just some random exile. He'd spoken to the guards with familiarity. He'd mentioned Jadirel's desires like he had inside information. And his quarters were nicer than the squalor she'd seen on display while walking through Jadirel's exile kingdom the day before.

This man had some kind of status. She could use him. And if he didn't know where her sister was, he could find out information. Layala had been her only contact on Guerran. If Kenzie played her cards right, Mad might help her, too.

What was his price? Her body? She'd given that freely. Or perhaps fear for his life would be enough to make him talk.

She pulled the knife back enough to give him room to speak, but pressed her *other* knife against his side before he could take advantage of the movement. If he fought back, she could disembowel him before he overpowered her. Maybe he'd kill her before he died, but he'd pay for it with his life.

"I should have known you'd be deadly," he said, eyes dancing and lips quirked up like he couldn't quite suppress a grin. "You could be a star in the pit."

"I'd rather swim in shit." She couldn't keep the venom out of her voice. She fought because she had to, not for some spectacle. Yes, she'd climb into that pit night after night if it meant she could find Carise. But she'd never do it out of some misguided search for fame and fortune.

"What do you want?" Mad asked. His eyes flicked to her knife, and she felt his muscles tense. She let the tip of the knife on his side bite into flesh.

He froze.

There was no time to waste. He could have friends coming, he could be expected somewhere. He could scream. She needed to speak.

"My sister Carise was brought to Guerran sometime in the last two months. She may have been purchased as a slave for Jadirel three weeks ago. I went to his palace to find out, and he made me fight in the pit. He said he hadn't purchased Carise, but I have no reason to believe him. I want you to tell me everything you know about his slaves and his palace." Perched as she was, she couldn't forget the strength of his body, but she was trying to ignore it.

Why was it so difficult?

"Why do you think I know anything?" Mad asked, far more calm than the situation warranted.

He was stalling. He had to be. But she didn't stab him again. There was only so much she could do before she'd have to resort to torture. She'd never tortured a man before.

She didn't need any more firsts today.

"You said you didn't want me in Jadirel's bed." The way he'd said it had set her body alight, and she was trying not to picture it. Trying and failing.

"And?" For a man with a knife at his throat, he seemed too comfortable.

Should she be insulted?

"It means you knew he wanted me there. I saw you sitting beside him in the pit. You know the man. And you don't like him. Helping me will piss him off. It may be petty revenge, but at least it's something." She couldn't offer him many credits, so she didn't try.

"Seeing as you have the knives, I'll talk. He has two *favorite*," he scowled at the word, "humans. He keeps them on chains in his throne room. There are probably others. He used to have different favorites, but I assume they're dead now. Perhaps he sold them. I haven't seen any new humans in the last two months." He paused for a moment, seeming to think over what he was about to say before continuing. "I know one of the guards at the slave market. I might be able to sneak in and check the books. If your sister was sold there, there's a transaction record. We may not have laws here, but the slavers are always sure to get paid."

"You'll help me?" She didn't mean to sound so

disbelieving. Then again, she wasn't the type who'd help a person holding her at knifepoint.

"Slavers are a blight. As for you..." He grinned, and though it had to be a trick of the light, his eyes seemed to glow. "Yes, I'll help you."

"Why?"

He moved faster than she could counter, arching his hips up, bucking her off balance, and going for her knives. He hit a pressure point on her wrist and she lost her grip on the knife on his throat, making it clatter to the floor. She didn't give up the second knife so easily, but he pulled her arm away and flipped her over until he was flat on top of her, his breath hot on her neck.

And his cock hard against her back.

"Do you want me to back away?" he asked, the question somehow both a threat and a promise.

His lips caressed the back of her neck, and she shivered. He'd put some erotic spell on her and she was powerless. He'd let her hold those knives to him; to him it was foreplay.

And Kenzie's own body was tight with want.

Her mouth opened, ready to beg him for more, when someone banged on his door.

Mad jerked back.

"Open up!" a sort of familiar male voice demanded.

Mad cursed. "It's Tyze. One of Jadirel's men. Hide if you don't want to be captured." Then he raised his voice towards the door. "Give me a minute, I'm coming."

Kenzie scrambled off the bed and reached for her fallen knife.

9

MAD DIDN'T WATCH TO SEE WHERE KENZIE HID. IF HE knew, he might give her away, not that there were many options in his quarters. He pulled on a long tunic and wiped at the blood on his neck. There wasn't much of it, and hopefully Tyze wouldn't ask questions. There were plenty of reasons a man on Guerran might be bleeding.

Why did he tell her to hide? She'd been ready to use that knife. She wasn't his woman, wasn't his *mate*. Whatever madness had taken them over the night before couldn't influence his decisions. He didn't normally allow people to get away with holding a knife to his throat.

But if it weren't for Tyze's terrible timing, Mad's cock would be buried to the hilt in Kenzie.

For some reason he liked her knives. He wanted

to see her use them again. But not on him.

He *couldn't* think about her while Tyze was in front of him. His face would give him away, and the man would do whatever it took to drag her before Jadirel. The king got what the king wanted, and once Jadirel had his hands on Kenzie, he'd suck her dry of her energy before he let her go.

Power brimmed inside of Mad, and for the first time in a long time, his soul didn't hunger for Krudare. He'd fed on the energy he and Kenzie created while they fucked. She didn't seem any worse for wear. But he needed to be careful. It couldn't happen again. No matter how much he wanted her.

Tyze pounded on the door again. Before long, he'd try to break the thing down.

Mad hoped he'd bought enough time for Kenzie to hide. There weren't many options in his quarters. Under the bed or in the wardrobe, he'd guess. Perhaps out on the balcony. He couldn't check. She was a clever woman, he had to trust her. She'd survived this long without him.

Mad opened the door and nearly got pounded in the head by Tyze's fist. The man pulled back just in time.

He *looked* like he hadn't slept. His face was gaunt and he was low on energy. If he fought Mad,

Tyze would know Mad was stronger than usual. So it couldn't come to that.

Tyze shouldered his way past Mad and looked around the room. "The girl from the pit, where is she? The guards said you took her for the king."

Mad *really* hoped Kenzie didn't hear that part. Her knife was sharp. Maybe if he kissed her, she'd give him a chance to explain.

"She wasn't happy to return to King Jadirel," Mad said, not *exactly* lying. "Her knife stings. She nearly gutted me." He would have lifted his tunic to show where Kenzie's knife had left him bleeding, but the wound was barely clotted, and he didn't want to show Tyze his dick.

Tyze narrowed his eyes and looked around the room again, staring into emptiness as if it would reveal secrets. "She's human, hardly a match for you. I've seen you fight."

"She took out Baryn with no trouble." Mad could beat Kenzie in a fight, but he'd pay for it in blood and pain. And he didn't want to fight her. Not when there were more pleasurable options.

"You're not Baryn." Tyze yanked Mad's wardrobe open, his free hand prepared to grab for a fleeing woman, but Kenzie wasn't hiding there.

Mad didn't look at the bed. He was crazy for trying to protect her, but he didn't want Tyze to take her to Jadirel. She was right; he didn't like the exile king, and he certainly didn't want her in the man's clutches.

But would he fight Tyze for her? Would he openly oppose Jadirel?

He was scared to think too hard about it. The answer could be yes. And a yes was suicidal.

"Are you done chasing shadows?" Mad tried to sound bored, as if this invasion of his privacy was nothing more than an annoyance.

Tyze looked into Mad's bathing room and then scowled back at Mad when it was empty. Did the man expect Kenzie to be hiding in the plumbing?

She had to be under the bed. When Tyze turned away, Mad tried to see if he could spot her. He kicked a dirty tunic towards the gap under the bed, hoping to block it so that Tyze couldn't see. She had no place to run.

His axe was on the other side of the room, right by his small kitchen area, which consisted of a cold storage box for his food and a small area he could light a fire to boil water or heat food.

Mad walked to the kitchen as casually as he could. "Would you like tea?" he asked Tyze as he poured water into the kettle and started the flame.

Tyze scowled at him and looked in the wardrobe again, this time pulling out Mad's clothes and throwing them on the bed. "I don't have time for tea."

"Do you have time to put my clothes back where they belong?" he asked dryly.

Tyze glared.

Mad let the water boil. It was another potential weapon against Tyze. But the bed was between them, and if Mad bent over and grabbed his axe, it was a declaration of intent. He couldn't touch an obvious weapon while Tyze was looking for Kenzie.

Tyze sank to his knees beside the bed, and Mad held his breath. The kettle boiled and he grabbed the handle, ready to throw the whole thing at his opponent.

Then Tyze stood up with a frustrated grunt, clearly disappointed. And empty handed. "If you see that human, bring her to the king. You'd be doing yourself a favor. She's not worth your life."

Tyze stomped out of Mad's room, and Mad carefully closed the door behind him after setting down the kettle.

Tyze had looked everywhere in the room. The whole of the balcony was visible from beside the bed, so it wasn't like he had to go outside to see that no one was hiding there. Still, Mad retraced the man's steps, looking in the wardrobe, the bathing room, and under the bed.

Kenzie wasn't there.

How?

He was on the third floor of this building. Climbing down from the balcony was suicide. Mad stepped onto the balcony and looked around, as if the human would appear out of nowhere.

She wasn't hanging from the side of the building.

But there was a smudge on the railing that surrounded the balcony. And another smudge on the drainpipe.

Mad looked up. It wouldn't be impossible to make it to the roof. Was that where his human had gone?

He retreated back into his rooms and saw her clothes half hidden in a pile of his own leathers. If Tyze had been paying attention, he might have noticed them, but he'd been so focused on finding the woman herself he'd ignored evidence that she'd been there.

Mad sent a prayer of thanks to the stars. That was one small favor.

He pulled on his own clothes and his leathers and then spread her clothes on the bed, searching through her pockets for any hint of her.

Orion was a big city, but Mad knew it well.

His human couldn't hide from him forever.

10

K ENZIE WAS BAREFOOT, AND THE TUNIC SHE'D STOLEN from Mad draped over her like a dress that hung past her knees. She'd had to leave one of her knives behind, but she still had her favorite blade. She felt half naked with just the one blade and no underwear. She'd live.

Her feet were torn up, and she hoped she wasn't bleeding. In her head, she made a list of the things she needed: more weapons, shoes, better clothes.

Food.

Ignoring her grumbling stomach, Kenzie planned. Guerran wasn't safe, especially with people looking for her.

She's managed to snag a piece of rope that was lying on Mad's roof and had fashioned a belt out of it, cinching her waist in so the tunic felt a bit less likely to wave in the wind and make her flash everyone.

She still felt naked. And she smelled like Mad.

It was probably the shirt. She *hoped* it was the shirt. But she knew he was embedded in her skin after last night. His masculine scent enveloped her and made her yearn. Her body remembered every second of it and wanted to go back for more.

But Kenzie wasn't on Guerran to find a man. She had to find her sister.

Luckily, she hadn't abandoned all of her things in Mad's apartment. She'd stashed her bag in a place Layala had claimed was safe enough for storage. She had to hope the woman was right about that.

Unfortunately, it was halfway across the territory, and she'd have to cross a good deal of the city to get there. Probably for the best. She didn't know what Mad would tell King Jadirel's man. There was a good chance he sold her out the second he opened the door.

Then why had he told her to hide?

Ugh! *This* was why she didn't get involved. It screwed up her brain and made her think of things other than what she was supposed to be doing. Carise was all that mattered. Kenzie didn't *get* to have fun flings with sexy alien men. All that did was lead to distraction and betrayal.

She'd failed Carise once, she couldn't do it again.

She slowed to a walk as she weaved through Jadirel's territory. The streets were bustling today, with stalls lining the narrow road and people milling around.

Market day.

It gave her cover, but made moving more difficult. She couldn't run. Running drew too much attention. So she walked and smiled and played the role of a happy woman on her shopping day.

No one cared that she didn't wear shoes. She wasn't the only barefoot shopper. Shoes seemed to be a luxury around here. At least the city was warm enough that her feet didn't freeze. But she was going to have dirt embedded in her skin for weeks.

Her mind skipped ahead to her next step after she resupplied. She had two options: sneak into the slave market and try and find their records, or sneak into Jadirel's compound to see if Carise was there.

Her instincts screamed at her that Jadirel was the one to go after. He kept people on their knees and in chains. There was nothing stopping him from purchasing her sister and... using her.

Kenzie shivered. She didn't want to think of what he could be doing to Carise right then. She spent a good portion of her time forcing herself *not* to think of the horrors her baby sister could be suffering. That way led to despair and hopelessness. The first months of her journey, she'd had nightmares every night about the things slavers might do to Carise. It had taken a lot of work to push that out of her mind. Dwelling on it wouldn't help.

As long as Carise was alive, she could be saved. They'd deal with the fallout afterwards.

Jadirel said he didn't have Carise, but he was probably a liar. Mad said he hadn't seen Carise, but he didn't have the access he would need to confirm that. She needed to get in to check.

But she didn't want to get captured as a way in. That would leave her too vulnerable and make it that much harder to sneak out. No, Kenzie had to find a way to sneak in, see if Carise was there, and get out without being detected.

Easy peasy.

She hated Guerran already. Some of the planets she'd skipped across on her search to find Carise had been almost pleasant. This was a place of violence full of barbarians who'd sooner hold a woman captive than answer her questions.

But the men *were* hot.

No! She had to put Mad out of her mind. Last night was a bit of insanity that could not be repeated under any circumstances. She'd almost compromised her entire mission. She couldn't put her trust in that man. He was close enough to Jadirel to sit beside him at the fights. That meant he was a danger to Kenzie.

It didn't matter how safe she felt in his arms.

She thumped her palm against her forehead as if that would knock some sense into her. It didn't do anything.

Her stomach grumbled, and she realized she hadn't eaten anything since her meeting with Layala. There'd been food set aside for the fighters, but she'd been concerned it might have been drugged, so she kept away.

A full day without a meal made her grouchy. She *could* go longer if she had to, but a fed warrior was a competent warrior.

Delicious smells wafted from a few of the tents in the market. There'd been a few credits in her pockets, more than enough for a meal, but Kenzie's clothes were back on Mad's floor. The only thing of value she had was her knife, and she wasn't about to barter that.

She patted the tunic down, hoping to find a pocket, and had to bite back a cry of triumph when she found one with three small coins inside of it. They were crude and likely minted on Guerran, but she was pretty sure she had enough to purchase something to fill her stomach.

Breakfast and then supplies.

Her plan made, she wandered off towards the best smelling tent and made it halfway there before a giant of a Kru'dari bumped into her and nearly sent her sprawling to the ground.

He mumbled what might have been an apology before turning towards a tent filled with frilly, colorful dresses.

He didn't look like the frilly, colorful dress type.

She glared after him as he pawed through dresses small enough for a person half his size.

Kenzie turned away. There was no reason to start a fight, especially not with the biggest Kru'dari in the market. She had to get food and get away. Mad could be chasing after her at any minute.

Her thoughts must have summoned him.

"Jaek! Hey!" he called out. It wasn't her name, but the man by the dresses stiffened before stepping to the stall beside the dresses, which was selling all sorts of figurines.

Kenzie melted into the shadows behind the stalls. Breakfast would have to wait. She needed to get out of sight before Mad saw her and she ended up in even more trouble.

Or back in his bed.

11

"JAEK!" MAD CALLED AGAIN, SURPRISED TO SEE HIS FRIEND in the marketplace. Jaek hated market days and did his best to avoid them, usually paying one of the children milling around the territory to purchase things he needed and deliver them to him. And yet here he was, gazing at figurines like he'd never seen anything more interesting.

Jaek finally turned around and grunted a greeting.

Ah, yes, Jaek was in a characteristically sour mood. Wonderful. "Did you get my message?"

Jaek shrugged and turned from the figurines to face the market. As Mad looked at him, he noticed that Jaek looked different than normal. Not cleaner, exactly, but more *groomed*. As if he'd taken time to tame his beard and his braids and chose a tunic that hadn't been once spattered in blood. Interesting.

Mad spotted Tyze walking among the crowd and hoped Tyze didn't see them. He turned so he was facing the figurines, right beside Jaek, and kept sneaking glances over his shoulder back at Jadirel's lieutenant.

At least Mad could try to fulfill his other job right now. "Jadirel's looking for you. Did you make him angry?" Mad knew he'd said the wrong thing when Jaek glared at him, but his friend didn't say anything. "Is everything alright?" Jaek was normally in a bad mood, but this was sour, even for him.

"Need to go home," he said, hand hovering over a figurine before pulling it back. The small statues really weren't his style. "Prom—" He cut himself off.

Mad could follow *that* thought, but he decided to play nice. "Did you need to get something from the market? I could deliver it for you." Jaek hated crowds, especially since his height and breadth made him a target for exiles who wanted to prove themselves. Taking on an exile of Jaek's size would prove to everyone that a man meant business.

But Jaek never lost a fight, no matter how much he wanted peace. Guerran made brutes out of everyone.

"It's fine," Jaek mumbled, and jerkily turned away from the table. "See you later." He melted into the crowd before Mad could stop him. And he still didn't know if Jaek was going to give in and go see Jadirel.

Everyone was running away from him today.

Kenzie couldn't have gotten far. Her clothes hadn't told him much, except that she was even more dangerous than she first appeared. He hadn't realized you could hide a weapon in the sleeve of a shirt, but he'd pulled on a thread and realized it could be used as a garotte.

She was ready for action, no matter what.

And Tyze was looking for her.

Mad had to find her first. Tyze wouldn't show mercy, and Kenzie was no match for him, no matter how many weapons she had. Tyze was a merciless butcher. He'd either slaughter her or drag her back to Jadirel half-broken. Even having seen Kenzie fight in the pit, she didn't stand a chance.

Mad had to stop that from happening.

But where was she?

Someone would have noticed a naked human running through the streets, so he assumed she'd found clothing somewhere. And since he wasn't the tidiest of Kru'dari, it was perfectly possible the clothing had come from his floor before she ducked out of his quarters. He'd found one of her knives, but he knew she'd had at least two. So she was armed.

But where?

A wave of awareness pulsed through the crowd around him, and Mad looked around. He didn't see Tyze. No one was screaming.

But *something* was happening.

People didn't scream on Guerran if they could help it. That only brought down the vultures. And everyone loved a fight.

Some extra sense he'd developed during his six years of exile tugged him into the makeshift alley between two rows of tents. A few exiles stared into the gloom, and it was quickly apparent why.

Tyze had someone cornered.

Tyze had *Kenzie* cornered.

Mad was moving before he could think better of it. The only thought in his head was that he had to protect his woman. Energy burbled within him, stronger than it should have been. He could think about the why of it later, but right now he stalked towards the fight with an unholy determination.

Kenzie had her back to a building, her knife out in front of her and a violent light in her eyes. She was wearing one of his tunics, and at another time,

Mad would have let himself enjoy the thought of his woman in his clothes.

He grabbed his axe and stepped into the fight. This was no time to fight fair, and if it weren't for the crowds and the bunched up stalls, he might have been able to get behind Tyze and take him out before the exile knew he was there.

Mad swung his axe, and Tyze tipped his head back and laughed. "You utter fool," he spat at Mad. "You're throwing away your life."

Mad didn't speak. Tyze had a short sword and he knew how to use it. He loved taunting his opponents into making mistakes. The only way to beat him was to ignore every word he said.

Even if he was right.

Word would get out about this fight. No one would blame him for killing Tyze. But doing it to save Kenzie might cost him everything.

Mad didn't care. Every one of his instincts screamed at him that Kenzie was important, was worth it. His instincts had steered him wrong before. They were the reason he'd ended up on Guerran in the first place.

But that didn't mean instinct should be ignored.

He fell into the fight, dodging Tyze's blows and swinging his axe with the kind of fury that only came from knowing he was in a fight for the death. Tyze was just as skilled as he was, and meaner too. But Mad was motivated.

Tyze couldn't have Kenzie.

Tyze came at him in a flurry, but it only took one lucky blow of Mad's axe to end it all. Tyze fell to his knees, and the energy within him swirled close to the surface, beginning to drain out with all of his lifeblood.

He wasn't dead, not quite yet, but he wasn't going to make it.

His eyes locked with Mad, and there was only confusion and anger. Tyze hadn't gone out today thinking he would die.

But that was life on Guerran.

Mad kicked Tyze's sword to the side and grabbed the leather strap around Tyze's chest, yanking him up. He held Tyze close and breathed in his energy. He noticed the acrid smell of death as Tyze's life seeped out of him, but his energy was what nearly overwhelmed Mad. Some of it was lost through his wound. If Mad were desperate, he might have smothered himself in the blood to collect as much as he could.

As the energy abated, Mad let Tyze fall. The crowd around them had dispersed. Someone was bound to tell Jadirel sooner or later, but Mad would deal with that then.

He turned around and saw Kenzie right where Tyze had cornered her, a hand around her knife and a heated glare on her face.

12

The alien was a vampire. Or, at least, he looked like one with his face buried against his victim's neck.

His hands were covered in blood and a little was smudged on his face. Now would be the time for Kenzie to run. If she wasn't so desperate to find her sister, she'd be on the next transport off of Guerran.

But Carise was here.

And Kenzie was more likely to stab the stupid alien vampire in front of her rather than run from him.

"Why'd you have to kill him?" she demanded. If she was just a little more reckless, she might have shoved at him. As it was, she put her knife away and kept glaring.

Mad blinked twice, as if he was confused. "Excuse me?"

"Why. Did. You. Kill. Him?" She emphasized every word, speaking slowly, just in case her translator was working on a delay.

But, no, Mad stared at her in disbelief as he wiped off his axe and placed it back in its holster. "He was going to drag you to Jadirel. I was protecting you."

"I don't need protection." Okay, that was maybe a lie. She hadn't been confident she could face off against Tyze, but she was willing to try. She found people liked to answer questions when the other option was getting stabbed a lot. "I was going to interrogate him."

"Before or after he beat you to a pulp?" Mad stepped close. He was cut up and blood covered, and he should have been disgusting.

Why did Kenzie want to kiss him?

She knew how good he tasted, what his body felt like when he was as close as he could be. Wasn't fucking a guy supposed to get him out of her system? So why did she want to drag him deeper into the shadows and have her way with him again?

This planet was crazy.

"I had him right where I wanted," she said. A wise woman would have her knife out for this conversation. But she was far from wise when it came to Mad.

"He won't help you, but I will. Come on. Someone's going to come for his body, and we don't want to be here when that happens." He nodded further down the alley between the tents and took off.

Kenzie followed him. Why did she want to trust him? He was a criminal. She'd had a knife to his throat and threatened him to get information. And instead of trying to get payback, he'd protected her. It didn't make any sense.

Very little in Kenzie's life made sense these days. And she needed help.

When she caught up to Mad, he was speaking with a stall owner and handing over a few coins in return for a package that smelled like bread and meat. The vendor didn't seem to notice that Mad was covered in blood.

This was a fucked up place.

Once Mad was done with the vendor, he turned to her. "Let's get off the streets for a while."

She kept following him and was a little surprised when he led her right back to his quarters. "Aren't the..." Well, not cops, there weren't cops on Guerran. "Isn't someone going to come after you for that guy's death?"

An emotion she couldn't read danced across Mad's face, but he quickly hid it. "I'll be fine," he assured her. "I may have just given myself a promotion."

"What?"

He shrugged. "Tyze's death upsets the power structure among Jadirel's people. He may give me more responsibility. Fuck." Mad set the food down on the table. "Eat, you must be starving. And wait here while I wash off. Your things are on the bed."

Kenzie didn't look at the bed. Looking there would remind her of everything they did last night, and that way lay madness. Her stomach was about to stage a revolt, so she grabbed the food and dug in. It wasn't like Mad could have poisoned it. Besides, she was in his quarters already and a bit at his mercy.

Had he let her get the upper hand?

She chewed slowly as she thought it over. The fight with Tyze had been brutal and quick. Mad used his axe like he'd been born with it, a barbarian exile who lived for violence. He was stronger than her in every conceivable way. And yet he'd let her hold two knives on him. He'd only resisted when Tyze showed up at the door.

Why?

She didn't like the thought that she was being humored. Part of her wanted to march into his bathroom and demand an explanation. But Kenzie wasn't stupid. She stuffed the rest of the food in her mouth and finished it.

At some point Mad had decided to let her hold a knife to his throat. For the first minute or so, he might have been laying there and assessing the situation, but after that he'd decided that it was better to appease her than to fight. She didn't know if he was playing a game or if he was really on her side.

It would be foolish to trust him.

But she already did. She'd followed him back to his apartment. She'd eaten the food he'd given her, and she was waiting while he wiped off the blood he'd spilled protecting her.

Meal finished, Kenzie grabbed her clothes off the bed and quickly changed into them. She was thankful to have her shoes back and wasn't *at all* disappointed that she was no longer wearing a tunic that smelled like Mad.

Who was she trying to kid?

Mad came out of the shower wearing nothing, and Kenzie had to bite her tongue to keep from making a noise. Did they not have towels on Guerran?

She couldn't help staring at his tight ass while he picked clothes out of his wardrobe and pulled them on. She forced herself to look away before he turned around and caught her. But from the way he grinned, he knew what he did to her.

"Satisfied?" he asked.

"What?" Her cheeks heated and she hoped she wasn't blushing. Maybe he wouldn't notice.

His grin widened. "Your food. Would you like more?"

She shook her head, trying to push aside her nerves. She was almost thirty years old, not some blushing child. "I'm good. Thanks."

Mad took pity on her and stopped teasing. "As we discussed this morning before we were interrupted, I'll go to the slave market and check the records. Do you have an image of your sister? Can you give me a description?"

"Yes." Kenzie stretched her arm out and bunched up the fabric around her elbow. She ran her finger over the sensitive skin over her forearm and tapped out a familiar pattern.

Mad watched the way her fingers moved, but if he was curious about what she was doing, he didn't say anything. Smart man.

A dark line appeared on her arm, followed by another, then another. A shape started to form, and after a minute her sister's face was there, tattooed on her arm where she belonged.

"I've had to ditch all my things more than once. I

used to carry photos of Carise with me, but after I risked my life twice to get the photos before moving onto another planet, I realized I needed a better way to carry her with me. I got a specialist in the Oscavian Empire to make the disappearing tattoo. It's keyed to a special code. That way I get to choose who sees Carise. Wearing her on my skin all the time could be dangerous. I don't want her to get hurt because of me. Take a good look." Kenzie held her arm out so Mad could look his fill.

It was intimate. Too intimate. Especially when he held her wrist in his giant hand and took his time studying her sister.

"She looks like you," he said. His eyes flicked up, and her heart flipped. Before he let go of her hand, he kissed the inside of her wrist.

Kenzie pulled her arm away as if she'd been burned. "People thought she was my clone when we were little, she looked so much like me. It changed as we got older. But faces don't lie. Will you remember what she looks like?"

Mad nodded in solemn promise.

Kenzie ran her fingers over her arm, and the tattoo disappeared. "When can you check the records at the auction house?" She needed to *move*. She'd been sitting around doing nothing for far too long, and she hated the thought that Carise might be suffering at someone's hands somewhere.

"I need to speak with Jadirel about Tyze. If I'm lucky, I'll be able to get into the auction house tonight. Tomorrow morning at the latest. I'll try to look through Jadirel's people as well, just to ensure your sister isn't there. We can meet tomorrow, but not here."

"Will your quarters be watched?" Kenzie didn't look forward to fighting more Kru'dari, but she'd do it if she had to.

Mad shrugged. "Perhaps. There's a restaurant not far from here. The White Flower. Let's meet there."

"Fine. Tomorrow." Kenzie stood. She had to get out of Mad's apartment before she did something stupid, like pull him down to the bed to while away the afternoon.

Mad stood with her. They were close, only a foot or so separating them. Their eyes locked, and she was sure he was going to kiss her. If he did, she wouldn't be able to resist.

She wanted it so bad her heart hurt.

Mad stood between her and the door. Kenzie gave him a nod and backed out until she was on the balcony. She stepped onto the railing and vaulted up, grabbing a drain pipe and hauling herself onto the roof, leaving the same way she'd left that morning.

Mad didn't follow.

She tried not to feel disappointed.

13

MAD COULDN'T SPEND THE DAY WISHING HE'D PULLED Kenzie into his bed and kept her there. By now, someone had surely told Jadirel about the fight with Tyze, and if he didn't report to the king soon, he'd be in danger.

He *was* in danger.

Tyze had been a favorite of the exile king. Killing a favorite came with consequences. But Mad could deal with that. What other choice did he have? He was the only person standing between Kenzie and Jadirel, and he was going to make sure the exile king did not get his hands on her. He'd lie straight to Jadirel's face and kill anyone the man sent after him.

But why? Some need to protect the human pulsed in him, and Mad couldn't question it. Something in her called to him. Her energy swirled around in his veins. All he knew was that he needed more from her. And if he could protect *anyone* from Jadirel, he'd call it a win.

Mad dressed carefully for the meeting. He had to exude strength without posing a direct threat. He put on his leathers and took his axe. Most days he could get away with just a knife, but these days things were too dangerous. More and more people were being exiled, and the streets were getting crowded with wannabe tough guys. Mad didn't have time to fight. He needed something that could kill in a single blow.

No one bothered him on his walk to Jadirel's palace, though there were plenty of not so furtive whispers. News of the fight had spread. Mad wasn't a champion fighter, and if he'd faced Tyze in the pit, the bets would have been against him.

And yet Mad was the one alive right now.

Mad braced himself as he entered. The guards at the door let him through without any issue, and when he made it to the throne room, Jadirel was alone. Mad didn't know if that was a good thing or a bad thing. Jadirel liked to punish his people in public, but executions were often private.

Had Mad walked to his death?

He took off his axe and placed it near the entrance as a sign of good faith. A Kru'dari could not approach his king armed with a deadly weapon, not unless the king was absolutely sure of his loyalty.

Or unless the Kru'dari had murderous intent.

Not even the chained humans were in the room with Jadirel. This *was* serious.

Jadirel waved his hand, and the door to the throne room slammed shut. Neat trick. Since telekinesis wasn't a Kru'dari power, there must have been a hidden sensor or someone waiting for his signal.

"I wanted the human brought to me." Jadirel's words cut Mad like glass. "Were you so dull you couldn't understand a simple request?"

Now was not the time to argue technicalities. Mad went to one knee and bowed his head.

He sensed the blow coming right before Jadirel kicked him in the stomach. Mad refused to fall over. He didn't know if he was being foolish or not.

"Tyze was an asset, you fool!" The king kicked him again, and Mad couldn't hold back the grunt of pain. That was what it took to satisfy the king. He stepped back. "Stand up."

Mad stood, trying not to wince.

"He was an asset," Jadirel repeated, "and ambitious. My spies say he was getting ready to challenge me. You've never wanted the throne."

"No, sir." That Mad could admit with absolute

certainty. It took a certain level of ruthlessness to rule as an exile king. All he wanted was to go home.

Jadirel clapped once. "Wonderful!" He slouched back onto his throne. "Then let's make something clear, I own you. When I tell you to bring me a girl, you bring her to me. When I tell you to fight, you fight. When I tell you to kill, you bring me my enemy's head. Do you understand?"

Mad had to swallow hard before he could force the words out. "Yes, sir." He hated being here. He hated how small Jadirel made him feel. He was only six steps from his axe. If he was swift enough, he could end this all.

But Jadirel wasn't a fool. And he wouldn't be sitting alone with Mad if he didn't have some sort of extra protection.

"Find the human and bring her to me, is that clear enough?"

Mad stood on a precipice. Before this moment, he'd been able to dodge some of Jadirel's orders, but he did his best to not outright lie to the king. He didn't want to be accused of challenging the man in any way.

But this would be a challenge. A Kru'dari more concerned with his own survival would abandon Kenzie to Jadirel.

Mad's whole soul rebelled at the thought.

"Yes, sir," he lied. And then another thought occurred to him. He had to be careful. Subterfuge didn't come easy to him, and Jadirel had been an exile king for a long time. He expected plots. But this was an opportunity to find out more about Carise. "I spoke to Tyze before he died. He said the girl had been ranting about a lost sister." He sent up a silent apology, as if Kenzie could hear him speaking, but he tried to keep his tone even. "She seemed to think you had her. If you do, I could use her as bait to get the girl to come out of hiding."

Jadirel gave him a look that Mad couldn't read. Whatever he was thinking, he didn't say. "She asked me about the sister. I've no need for more humans right now. But it *would* be convenient to have them both."

If Mad pushed, Jadirel would want to know why Mad didn't trust him. And at the moment, the king had no reason to lie.

Before Mad could figure out how to ask for more, Jadirel spoke. "Check with the slave auction. If she came through there, they'll know. I'll have eyes out on the streets looking for this girl. How hard could it be to find one human? Bring the fighter in. I'll find her sister. I'm sure they'll be happy to be reunited in my cages."

Mad had to keep his expression aggressively

neutral. He had to find Kenzie *and* Carise before Jadirel's spies spotted them. And he had to get them off of Guerran before they were dragged into Jadirel's palace. He had to make sure Kenzie stayed out of Jadirel's territory, but convincing her of that if there was even a whisper of her sister would be impossible.

That was a problem for later.

"I will check with the auction. I will not fail, sir." He wouldn't fail Kenzie.

Whatever it meant, he wouldn't. He didn't know why he was so called to her, but Mad couldn't betray her. He'd face consequences for it, but he'd gladly pay.

He remembered Arbyn's offer. He had his own way off the planet. Saving Kenzie and her sister could mean he'd have to give up everything.

It was a problem for later.

Mad bowed to Jadirel and retrieved his axe before heading to the auction house. He had a job to do.

14

WHILE MAD WAS LOOKING INTO THE AUCTION HOUSE, Kenzie retreated back to the cafe where she'd first met Layala. Her things were stashed near there, and she was probably safer outside of Jadirel's territory. He'd be looking for her, and she didn't want to be caught.

What would Mad tell him?

Kenzie could worry about that all day, or she could push forward. Carise was *here*. She had to be. Layala had the picture of her. This was the closest Kenzie had come to her sister in years, and she refused to believe that she would miss her again.

She'd come close before. Three planets back, she'd arrived only a month after her sister had been moved on. Sometimes the trail was clear and easy to follow, other times it made no sense. Kenzie would find ownership records or security footage, and then other times, Carise would disappear as if she were a ghost.

Kenzie dreaded what dark place Carise would be dragged to if she left Guerran. There were planets far worse than this one, and she didn't want her sister on any of them.

Tea steamed in a cup in front of her, floral, fruity, and delicious. The tea was better here than the last hellhole, that was for certain. There was even a certain charm to the chaos and violence of Guerran. Kenzie might have liked it if Carise weren't in danger.

Layala slid into the seat beside her. Kenzie hadn't known how to contact her, but she figured Layala would show up eventually.

"You had a busy day," Layala observed, taking her own tea with a smile from a passing waitress. "Lots of people looking for you after last night. I thought I told you to stay away from Jadirel."

Kenzie took another sip of tea. "You thought he could have my sister. I had to find out."

Layala hummed in the back of her throat and tilted her head to the side. "I see."

"You see what?" She didn't like Layala's tone.

Layala didn't seem to care. "You're on a crusade.

If you die in this holy war, you'll be absolved from losing your sister in the first place."

Kenzie automatically reached for her knife and had to stop herself from pulling it. Layala had one hand under the table, and Kenzie would stake everything she owned on Layala being armed. Kenzie put both hands on the table. "If I die, my sister stays trapped in whatever hellhole she's stuck in. Dying isn't an option."

"Has it occurred to you that your sister could free herself? Or perhaps she already has? What if you find her and she's not what you expect?" Layala sipped her drink as if she wasn't cutting Kenzie with every word.

Sometimes her dreams of reuniting with Carise turned into nightmares where her sister sent Kenzie away, where she blamed Kenzie for her abduction or for taking so long to find her. Losing her sister was the worst thing that had ever happened to her. If she found Carise and Carise walked away...

Kenzie couldn't contemplate it. "Carise is a gentle person, she's never been a fighter."

"Fighting is *not* the only path to freedom." There was a history in that sentence.

"How did you end up here? There aren't many humans on Guerran." And there certainly weren't many humans who could offer the kind of information that Layala seemed to deal in.

"I took a journey of my own. But we're not here to talk about me. You need to find your sister and get off Guerran. Better yet, you need to just leave. You've already made an enemy of an exile king. He has allies and he will use his resources to find you. Rumor has it his second in command was murdered by another one of his soldier,s and now *that* soldier is after you. Madn Damari." Layala scowled at the name.

Kenzie's first instinct was to come to Mad's defense, but she kept her mouth shut. All she knew about Mad came from what she'd seen and what he'd told her. Layala would have a different perspective. She didn't need to know what Kenzie knew.

Not yet, at least.

"Tell me." She made the demand and tried not to feel like she was betraying Mad. That was ridiculous. She barely knew him.

Layala was happy to give her information. "He's been on Guerran about six years now. Exiled for treason. Something about the deaths of a dozen or more civilians. He has no loyalty to anyone and can't be trusted. I've seen him in the pit. He's not unstoppable. As a matter of fact, he lost his last fight. But when he's in a murdering mood, no one stands in his way. If he's moving up in Jadirel's ranks, it means he might have his eye on the throne. I don't know what he's planning, but I'll find out soon enough. If you see him, you run. You're no match for him."

Kenzie's knife felt heavy in its sheath. Now wasn't the time to say she'd already had him at her mercy. Or that he'd killed for her. The man Layala spoke of didn't sound at all like the Mad she'd met.

"Are you saying he was exiled for murdering civilians?" She didn't, *couldn't*, believe it. The Mad she knew...

But she didn't know him. Not really.

Layala sipped her tea again and waved at the waitress, motioning for more. "I don't know. It's difficult to get information from Krudare, and a lot of exiles try to leave their old lives and old crimes behind. But someone on Krudare wanted people to know what Damari did. Some of the documents from the investigation landed in friendly hands. Damari committed treason and a lot of people died. He's lucky he wasn't executed."

Kenzie wanted to push back from the table and storm out of the cafe... or slap Layala. She wanted to spring to Mad's defense. Her pulse beat so rapidly she could feel a headache coming on, and she was starting to sweat.

Had he done something to her?

Shit. Having sex with him had been a bad idea.

So why didn't she regret it?

"Are you alright?" Layala asked. "You seem a bit flushed."

Kenzie sipped her tea and tried to get her emotions under control. "I'm fine."

If Layala didn't believe her, she kept it to herself. "Things aren't safe on Guerran, especially not for you. If you're smart, you'll conclude your business as quickly as possible and get out."

"I'll be gone as soon as I find Carise, or find out where her trail leads next." Kenzie didn't care about her own safety, not as long as she survived. She could deal with injuries and fear. She just had to survive long enough to get her sister free.

"And what happens when the trail goes cold?" Layala asked the question mildly, as if she wasn't stabbing Kenzie with every word.

Kenzie didn't answer. She couldn't.

Layala sipped her own tea before setting down the empty cup and placing a few credits on the table. "Conclude your business swiftly, otherwise you're going to start owing favors." She turned to leave before looking back for a moment. "Good luck." Then she left Kenzie alone.

Good luck. Right. Kenzie was going to need it.

15

MAD TRIED NOT TO THINK ABOUT WHY HE'D TOSSED AND turned the night before. He'd spent most of his evenings alone on Guerran. Last night was no outlier.

But it was a night without Kenzie.

He truly was going mad if one night with a woman had spoiled him for sleeping alone. Especially when the woman greeted him with a knife to the throat. He'd much rather wake to breakfast. Or lips around his cock.

But he'd done his part, and now he got to see Kenzie again. Excitement surged in him and he couldn't quash it. He'd spent six years on Guerran with no purpose other than survival.

At least now he was helping someone.

Where was the someone he was supposed to be helping?

Mad got to the meeting spot early and made sure he wasn't followed. Jadirel wasn't the type to micromanage, but now that word had gotten out about Mad killing Tyze, there were others who'd be after him. Life was cutthroat on Guerran.

Had someone found Kenzie? Alarm surged, and his fingers ached to grab his axe and start busting heads.

Kenzie was *his*.

And there was the madness again.

Kenzie was her own. She was on a mission, and she'd be leaving the planet as soon as it was done. There was no future for them. They existed for this one moment of time, and then she'd be nothing more than a memory.

You could go with her.

The dangerous thought danced across his mind. To go with her was to sacrifice every hope he had for returning home. He didn't know the human. He couldn't give up on his family like that.

And yet...

Temptation waited.

Mad looked down the street, hoping to spot the human. She wasn't walking towards him. He didn't see her at all. He tried not to worry. If Jadirel had caught her, word would have reached Mad.

Of course, word could take a while to travel.

No. She hadn't been caught. He had to believe that.

Something pulled his gaze up, and he saw a figure on the roof across the street. It could have been anyone. They were wearing a hood and too far away from him to make out features. But something in the way the figure held themselves told Mad it was Kenzie.

He rushed across the street and up the stairs of the building before she could run away.

And there she was, dark cloak overhead, knives strapped exactly where he expected them, and a Guerran-style tunic covering the rest of her. He liked her better in his own clothes, but seeing her in the clothes of this land was almost as good.

"Trying to blend in?" he asked. "You're too short for it." Kru'dari towered over humans, at least as far as he'd seen of the humans on Guerran. There weren't many of them. Maybe the taller ones were hidden on another planet. But as it was, Mad was more than a head taller than Kenzie.

All the better to shield her from danger.

"Blending here isn't an issue. You should have

seen some of the places I've been." Her hand rested on one of her knives, and her eyes were wary.

"I'd love to hear a story." Mad had been born on Krudare and shipped off to Guerran shortly after his twenty-sixth birthday. He only knew stories of other planets. Kenzie had traveled the galaxy.

And he was sure she'd give up every experience if it meant getting her sister back.

Her fingers gripped the handle of her knife, but she didn't pull it out.

"So we're back to that. Are you ever going to trust me?" He could still feel the ghostly imprint of her knife against his throat. If she'd pressed just a little harder, he might still carry her mark.

And why did *that* thought send a jolt of awareness to his cock?

He'd worn simple clothes today rather than his fighting leathers. He'd wanted to blend in as best he could, and wool was far less remarkable than his usual getup. But these simple clothes hid nothing, and if he didn't get himself under control he'd be on full display for his human.

Not that he minded. He wanted her to remember him in all his glory.

"Can a person ever trust a traitor?" She dropped her hand from the knife, but the question stabbed him all the same.

"Someone's been telling stories." Mad had hoped he could have a quiet existence on Guerran, but news of his conviction traveled fast. By the time he'd landed on the planet, it seemed like everyone knew he was a cowardly traitor.

He'd forced himself not to care. But with Kenzie, he wanted her to know the truth. "I was given an order to kill civilians. Intelligence said one of the king's enemies was hiding in a small village. It was deemed safer to level the town rather than infiltrate to find the criminal. Things may have turned out alright for me if I quietly refused and spoke to my commander privately. Instead, I warned one of the villagers and they all dispersed. The army hunted them down one by one. I refused to participate. They threw me in a cell, and here I am. The traitor."

He wasn't ashamed of what he'd done, even if it had besmirched the Damari name. He had to have his own ethics, or he was worth nothing. But sometimes he wished he hadn't been sent out at all that day. If he hadn't been assigned to that unit, he wouldn't have rebelled.

Kenzie watched him silently. Half the roof was between them, but it was like they were in their own little world. Some soft sounds from the street below drifted up, but this building was taller than any of the surrounding structures. "You protected people and they labeled you a traitor." It wasn't a question.

"It may be hard to believe but—"

"It's not," she said, cutting him off. "Your planet isn't the only place with a fucked up idea of justice." She looked disillusioned, and Mad wanted to comfort her. He wanted to prove to her that not everything was a ruin of ideals and optimism.

A hard ask on Guerran.

Mad sucked in a ragged breath as the rest of her words rushed over him. "No one has believed me in a very long time." He took a step towards her, as if he was being dragged by a wild animal.

Kenzie seemed to brace herself and remained rooted in place. "You're doing something to me." She spat the words out past a mouth that didn't seem willing to speak them. "What's your aim?"

Mad didn't step back. If anything, her words only spurred him on. *Mate.* The temptation whispered through his head and wrapped chains around his soul. A fated mate was something almost unheard of on Guerran. Kru'dari could mate one another as a way to exchange energy without the hand of fate, but that wasn't what Mad was feeling.

No, he felt drawn to Kenzie in a way he couldn't completely comprehend. His cock was a steel rod in his pants, and if she gave a hint of want, he'd take her right there.

He needed her. He wanted her. He'd *had* her. But it wasn't enough. It never would be, not until she wore his mark and accepted she was his.

The possessive insanity should have made him back away. Kenzie didn't plan to stay on Guerran for long. She wasn't meant for him.

But fate was a fickle master.

"I'm not doing anything to you." His voice was gravelly.

Kenzie closed her eyes and swallowed hard. "What did you find out about my sister?" Her hands curled into fists and she leaned back.

Mad had to stay where he was. He didn't want her using one of her blades on him again. But he didn't step back. He wouldn't budge until she demanded it. "There was nothing in the auction house. No record of Carise."

She sucked in a breath and let it out. Another woman might have screamed. Kenzie's face was blank, not a hint of emotion, and Mad realized she must be holding on by a mere thread. If she let herself vent, she'd never stop screaming.

He wanted to hold her and tell her all would be well. But that wasn't a promise he could make. Not when her sister could be in some hellhole where myriad tortures awaited.

"Stop it!" Kenzie demanded.

"I'm not doing anything. You want answers? Ask the hand of fate." He didn't step closer. He didn't reach out to touch her. But it took iron hard control to stay rooted in place.

"This isn't me." She glared at him, teeth bared and ready for a fight. "I don't get *distracted*. You have to be doing something to me."

If he said he suspected she might be his mate, she would run, and he'd never see her again. Mad didn't need to be a psychic to know it was true. So he did the wiser thing and said nothing.

Kenzie lunged forward and kissed him.

16

She was possessed. Maybe the only way to exorcise this thing between them was to work it out. Physically. Excuses rushed through Kenzie's mind as she pressed herself tight against Mad. She needed release. He was close by. Her body liked his body. This was the last time and it would be out of her system.

None of them mattered. She was in Mad's arms and that was it.

She wanted him in a way she didn't understand. Whether this was its own kind of craziness, alien space pheromones, or years of pent up attraction spent on the first man too hot for her to resist, she didn't care. She was going to take Mad. Again.

And she was going to love every second of it.

He didn't try to push her away. Even better, he

gathered her in his arms and pulled her back from the ledge of the building. Probably for the best. When orgasm sent her soaring, she didn't want it to be literally. And that she trusted Mad to take care of her even in that small way should have scared her. But Kenzie was far away from fear.

She didn't have to be afraid when Mad was taking care of her. No one had taken care of her in so long, and if she wasn't careful, she'd get used to it. She could become addicted to this alien if she didn't watch herself.

But right then, she didn't want to behave. She couldn't if she tried.

There was a private alcove a few steps back that provided shelter from the heat of the day, and even better, a sitting area was set up with cleared ground and pillows. If she hadn't chosen this meeting place, she might have accused Mad of plotting.

But she was too caught up in kissing him to care. He could have fucked her up against a wall or under the glaring sun, and she would have loved it. That they had their own private alcove was an unexpected treat.

His clothes were thin wool and she was tempted to tear them off. Or maybe she could cut them with her knife. Mad got a hot look in his eyes when she went for her blades. Instead, she pulled and peeled his shirt off, revealing a chest she could write poems about if she had the skill. The muscle reminded her of warriors of old, and she wanted to memorize every inch of it... with her tongue.

How did a man get to be so fucking perfect?

Mad's lips trailed down her neck, teasing sensitive flesh and making her shiver. She felt strangely exposed. She never let anyone get this close, and here she was allowing this man to put his teeth on her neck. It wouldn't take much for him to kill her.

But judging by the hard flesh still trapped in his pants, killing her was the last thing on his mind. Not unless a person could be killed with pleasure.

He opened the laces of her tunic and exposed her breasts. The groan he let out at the sight made her shiver, and when he took one of her nipples in his mouth, she couldn't stop her gasp. Not that she wanted to. Her body was hot and tight, as if she didn't quite fit in her skin anymore, and the only way to make things right again was release.

She was surrendering to this thing between them, at least for now, and there was no reason to resist. Not anymore. If she was damning herself, at least she could enjoy it.

She ran her hand through Mad's hair, holding him in place, not that he wanted to pull away. The man's tongue was his weapon, and he was as much a warrior here as on the battlefield. But this time, she had no defense against him. He'd conquered her with his kisses.

It should have been a warning. He was barely doing anything to her, and yet she felt more pleasure than she could remember any lover ever giving her... except for Mad. It had to be more evidence of the crazy alien pheromones.

She'd stopped caring about that the second she kissed him.

He hiked up her tunic and she shimmied out of her underwear. The tunic had seemed practical when she put it on, and a distant part wondered if she'd always been planning for this.

When it was done, she'd deny it all. But now?

Yes, Kenzie could admit to herself just how much she wanted him, how much she'd hoped he would want her too. And he did. She couldn't wait to take him.

His finger teased her entrance, and she hitched her leg around his hip, giving him even more room. She wanted him buried inside of her. She hadn't forgotten the feel of him in the day since they'd been together. And she'd dreamed of him fucking her on their night apart.

She shouldn't have missed him. Missing him

was craziness. But every moment apart made her heart ache.

Now when they were tangled together like this, things felt right for the first time since their parting.

He stretched her, and thoughts of anything but the moment were washed away in a wave of pleasure. She was so close to coming already and she knew it could only get better.

How was it possible? How could a man that made her feel like this, who made her think about destiny and a future beyond her current path, have been born light years away from her?

What were the odds they'd ever meet?

She clutched him close, urging him inside. No matter how much she wanted this, they didn't have much time. And she *yearned*.

The blunt tip of Mad's cock brushed against her, and Kenzie gasped in pleasure, a gasp that transformed into a moan as he slowly slid inside of her. He filled her so thoroughly she knew she'd feel empty again until the next time she could take him to bed. And even though she shouldn't have been thinking about a future with him anywhere near her, in this moment she was helpless to stop.

They rocked together, hips pumping in a rhythm that was all their own. Kenzie had to choke back loud cries of pleasure. They were still on the roof.

The door wasn't locked. They could be walked in on at any moment.

That shouldn't have been hot. But somehow, the forbidden nature of this tryst made it all the better.

It sent her over the edge, and then her body was rippling around Mad's, holding him within her as she came. And he followed right after, his own sounds of pleasure music to her ears.

She breathed in his masculine scent as her body began to calm, her arms wrapped tightly around him.

They had to get back to business. She had to let him go.

In a minute.

She could steal just one more minute. And then she'd let herself think of everything that existed outside the cocoon of the two of them.

She just needed one more minute.

17

Mad had expected Kenzie to dart away from him as soon as her passion cooled. He'd been braced for the disappointment and half expecting another knife. When she'd let him pull her close and cuddle in the seating area's pillows instead, he'd had to hold back a self-satisfied smile.

They were making progress.

She'd smoothed her tunic down so she was mostly covered, though she hadn't done up the buttons all the way, and his hand itched to dip inside and cup her breast. He'd pulled up his own pants as well. If anyone walked in on them, a tryst might be suspected, but there was no proof.

Not much, anyway.

Kenzie leaned against Mad's chest, a welcome weight. She'd taken out one of her knives and was tracing a finger over the handle. Since she didn't seem keen to turn the blade on him, he'd call it progress.

"I should get back to looking for Carise," she said, but she didn't move to get up.

Mad wanted to wrap his arms around her and hold her in place. He was willing to bet all he was worth that Kenzie hadn't taken a full day for herself since she started looking for her sister.

Could he get her to take one hour?

He didn't hold her to him. If he tightened his grip, she'd pull away. That was her nature, he was beginning to understand. She could be coaxed, but never controlled. He'd have to remember that for the future.

If he could convince her they *had* a future.

"What did you mean?" She tilted her head up to look him in the face, green eyes wide.

"When?" He could get lost in her eyes, studying the way her pupils dilated, the shifting colors, the way they narrowed and assessed her targets.

"When you said I should ask the hand of fate? Is that a person? How superstitious is this place?" She put her knife back in its sheath and half turned in his embrace so she could look at him.

"Guerran doesn't have time for superstitions. There are a few temples to the gods, but they're mostly in the Green Zone. The gods live back on Krudare, and they don't care about exiles." He'd been a devout boy, happy to visit every temple as a child. But his faith had dried up as he grew. Guerran only made the loss more obvious.

Kenzie made a small noise, but didn't say anything.

"You don't want to engage in religious debate?" he asked with a smile.

Those eyes of hers got giant. "Hell no."

He laughed. "Fate isn't religious, at least not according to our scientists back home. It's a real force in the universe, though we can't directly see it. We *can* see how it affects things."

"So fate is like dark matter?"

"Perhaps." He was dancing up to the edge of what he suspected, that fate had brought Kenzie to him, that she was his mate. His true mate, not just some person he could choose to bond with. But he was learning how to read her, and the expression on her face was doubtful.

She didn't believe in fate, not yet. And he could not push her in a single conversation. He had to change the subject before she latched onto it.

"How did you become so skilled with weapons?" He didn't want to feel the kiss of her blade again, but he'd watch her fight all day... if he had some guarantee she wouldn't be hurt.

Kenzie was quiet for a long moment, and he thought she wouldn't let him get away with changing the subject. But she did. Eventually. "I learned to fight back on Earth. My own bullies at first, then Carise's. Our mom died when Carise was just a baby, and our dad was... useless. He didn't care that the neighborhood we lived in was getting rougher and rougher. I came home with a broken arm once, and he didn't even notice."

She paused, and Mad realized he'd made a noise. "That is unacceptable." He tightened his grip on her, just a bit. "I'd hunt down anyone who tried to harm you."

She studied him, eyes narrowed in concentration. And then she gave him a small nod. "It is what it is. The Detyen War made our town unlivable."

"There was a war?"

She shrugged. "Sort of? It happened mostly in space. But a detachment of aliens infiltrated our town to potentially use as a base, and a bunch of space junk crashed down and destroyed the local schools. They were just starting to consider rebuilding things when I left. Carise was nineteen, an adult. It should have been safe. I went to Earth-Col3 as a security officer and learned weapons skills.

I was there for five years. It was boring, but the pay was amazing. It should have set me up for life. We spent most of the time sparring each other rather than doing any work. And then I got home and everything changed. Carise was abducted, and it was all my fault."

"What? How?" There was no way that was possible. Mad may have not known Kenzie for long, but her love for her sister shined through with everything she was. She wouldn't let something like that happen.

This time Kenzie did sit up, and Mad couldn't hold her back. The space between them was an uncrossable chasm. "Carise was still a kid and I should have known that. Nineteen. She was practically still a baby. Dad had been making overtures, trying to be involved in helping her get a job or go to college. I thought maybe this time things would be okay. He didn't try with me, so maybe I was the issue. When I got back, she'd been gone for months. All Dad did was report her missing. He told me she probably ran off."

"It's not your fault." Mad couldn't hug her close, no matter how much he wanted, so he'd use his words as well as he could. "Are women commonly abducted from your planet? Was this something you even thought to be worried about?"

"It's common enough. A dozen or so confirmed abductions every year. Hundreds, maybe thousands, more suspected. There are billions of people on the planet, people get lost. I should have stuck around." Kenzie stood and began to button up her top.

"Twelve people out of *billions* are taken every year? She's just as likely to learn to fly as to fear abduction. It's not your fault." He got to his feet too. If Kenzie was about to run, he would chase. He wasn't letting her go with this guilt riding so close to the surface.

"You'd understand if you had a sister."

"I do." Mad could still picture Taiana's face as she'd visited him in his cell on his last night on Krudare. It didn't matter that he'd seen her through a screen dozens of times since then. Her fear and disappointment hung over his shoulders every day. "She's married to an ambitious leech back home. I would have protected her from him if I could, but he married her two months after I was sent here. I know it's not quite the same, but I'll go through any torture here on the hope that I can one day stand by her side again." He could leave it at that, but more words sprang up. "Arbyn arranged transport for me off Guerran."

She tilted her head in question. "You say that like it's a bad thing."

"If I leave Guerran, my exile can never be lifted. That's what keeps most of us here." It was a cruel punishment. Home was only a few hours away by shuttle, and there was a space port with plenty of ships. "Rather than plead my case with the king or a judge, Arbyn wants me gone for good. But as long as Taiana might need me, I'm here."

"I'd live in hell if it meant keeping Carise safe."

"Good." Mad shifted his mind to the task. He couldn't take Kenzie back to his bed and spend the whole day there, no matter how much he wanted to. "I know where we should go next."

<h1 style="text-align:center">18</h1>

MAD MADE KENZIE PUT HER HOOD BACK ON AND HOPED IT wouldn't draw attention to her. They had to cross a good portion of Orion, and he didn't want her recognized. If word got back to Jadirel, things would go poorly for both of them.

But word wouldn't get back to the exile king. Mad would kill anyone who tried.

He felt naked without his weapons, but Kenzie had knives enough for both of them, and she'd even offered one to him. She might not have realized it yet, but he wasn't giving it back. He would take as many tokens from his mate—his *suspected* mate—as he could.

The outside of Jaek's cave looked as abandoned as it always did, but Mad knocked anyway. There was no answer. He knocked harder. Was Jaek still in a sour mood?

But after a few minutes, Mad was willing to believe that Jaek truly wasn't home, and he let himself and Kenzie inside.

"Do you bring every girl to your... cave?" Kenzie asked, wiping her finger against the stone.

Mad grinned back at her. "My friend Jaek lives here. He's been on Guerran longer than I have and has a surprising number of contacts throughout the city. He might have heard something about Carise. If there's even the tiniest hint of a rumor, he can track it down."

"You met Jaek in the market after I left you, right?" She eyed Jaek's table, and Mad followed her gaze. Two tea cups.

"After you ran away, you mean?" There was a challenge in his words. He didn't want Kenzie running again, and especially not from him.

"A strategic retreat." She didn't touch anything, and Mad wondered if part of that was her training from her time in security.

"Yes, that was Jaek," he confirmed. He still didn't know why his friend had come to the market. It wasn't like him.

"He was looking at clothing for a person much smaller than him. Does he have a girlfriend?

Boyfriend?" She took a deep breath and braced herself before asking the next question. "Human slave?"

"Jaek would never." The denial was instant and absolute.

She held her hands up in surrender. "Okay. I believe you. So who's his partner?"

"He doesn't have a woman. Or anyone else." Mad couldn't remember Jaek *ever* staying with someone. He wasn't sure Jaek even cared about fucking. And he liked his privacy too much to let a lover into his home.

The clothes could have been nothing. People looked at random things in markets all the time. But there was evidence of another person in Jaek's space. And since Mad was Jaek's closest—really, only—friend, and he hadn't put out those tea cups, there had to be another person in Jaek's life.

One he hadn't told Mad about.

The blanket was rumpled on the couch again, and there was a small shawl hanging on the edge of the couch. Too small for Jaek. Mad picked it up.

"Can I see that?" Kenzie asked, leaving her investigation of the tea cups behind.

Mad handed it over.

She ran her fingers over the fabric and stopped when she came to a label subtly sewn in along the hem. "This was mass produced in the Oscavian Empire."

"Okay." Mad didn't know much about where his clothes came from. He got them in the market. Sometimes they had tags, sometimes they didn't. He didn't question it.

"We're way too far away for them to be supplying much to Guerran. Either this was a very expensive import... or someone who was near the Oscavian Empire at some point got it from there. I tracked Carise around the empire for almost six months." She held the fabric up to her face and smelled it. "It's clean."

He could see her mind working and knew the conclusion she'd come to. "That's no proof Carise was here. But if she was, there's no safer place on Guerran than with Jaek."

Her face grew fierce. "She's safest with *me*, not some criminal."

It stung. Even worse than that, it hurt. Kenzie didn't seem to realize or care that Mad and Jaek were no different. He knew her emotions were running high and that she was desperate. But he didn't need to take her insults.

"I'm just a criminal to you?" It was important to hide emotions on Guerran. Otherwise they'd be used against a person. But Mad didn't want to hide from Kenzie. He wanted her to understand.

Her brows furrowed. "That's not what I meant and you know it. Don't turn this around on me."

Before he could open his mouth to say something he'd regret, the front door burst open and Jaek stomped into the room, a dark storm of a look on his face. "What the fuck are you doing here?" he demanded. "And who's she?"

"I'm—"

Mad cut her off. He didn't want her leveling accusations against Jaek as well. "I'm helping Kenzie find her sister. She thinks she was dumped on Guerran in the last month or so. Do you know anything?"

Despite the evidence of another person sharing Jaek's space, the exile was alone. Mad didn't ask about the extra teacup or the shawl. He'd press if he had to, but not yet.

Anger was riding him fast and hard, and he had to get it under control. But Jaek didn't help.

"Haven't seen anyone," he practically growled, shoving Mad aside. "Get out."

19

This was some friend Mad had. Kenzie wanted to rush up to him and tell him he didn't get to lay hands on Mad, but considering Mad looked ready to burst, she stayed in place.

She wasn't wrong. Exiles *were* criminals. They'd been exiled from their home as punishment. If Jaek was here, he was most likely an exile. Krudare had declared him an outcast.

But so was Mad. And he'd only tried to save people.

What if Jaek was the same?

Life wasn't exactly fair back on Earth, and plenty of people went to jail when they were innocent or only guilty of ridiculous crimes. But that didn't change the fact that she knew Carise would be safest with her. How could anything else be true? She was Carise's big sister.

She studied Jaek as he stomped through the homey little cave. He was even bigger than Mad, both in breadth and height. Was he seven feet tall? Maybe more? They grew them big on Krudare.

A nasty scar cut through his eyebrow, missed his eye, and continued on down his cheek. His blond hair was long and messy, though some of it was held back with simple braids. He had no expression on his face, and it made her think of a caged lion she'd seen in a zoo once.

There was a killer under all of that indifference.

Carise was supposed to be safe with *him?* Jadirel might be the better bet.

Mad hadn't stopped talking to Jaek, asking him questions about Carise and dancing around the fact that there was evidence of a second person in this charming little cave.

If Carise was with Jaek, Kenzie had to get her away from him. There was no telling what he'd do to her defenseless little sister. Her fingers itched to go for one of her knives, but Kenzie forced herself to stay still.

She couldn't take Jaek in a fair fight. Only dirty tricks and surprise would work. She wasn't opposed to trying them, but that didn't mean she was going to pounce just yet.

Not until they knew whether he'd laid a hand on Carise.

"I don't even know what this girl looks like," Jaek ground out. He looked ready to take on an army, he was so big and angry. "Stop asking questions."

Kenzie could fix that. She smoothed her hand down her arm and marched across the room, shoving her forearm in Jaek's face. She didn't care how scary she looked when there was a chance he'd seen Carise. "How about now? Have you seen her?"

Jaek was frozen looking at Kenzie's arm, and his expression slipped. She couldn't read it, but he wasn't the cold killer anymore. No, he looked somehow even scarier.

Who the fuck was this guy? What had he done?

"I just want my sister back." She had to be calm. Mad said Jaek knew a lot of people on Guerran. Maybe his information network rivaled Layala's, and she could use as much information as she could get.

Kenzie could keep her cool around Jadirel. So she had to keep even more cool around Jaek. Besides, Mad trusted this guy. That made him better than the exile king.

She hoped.

"That's enough." Mad stepped between her and Jaek, and she pulled her arm back. "You don't need to touch her."

Jaek's fingers had hovered above Carise's image, but he hadn't touched her.

"This is my house." Jaek glared at Mad. "I can do what I want."

The two Kru'dari were standing close, and the testosterone in the air was thick enough to choke on. If Kenzie had a bucket of water, she might have dumped it over the two of them to distract them.

What was the issue here? Weren't they supposed to be friends?

She forced her way in between the two men and looked all the way up at Jaek. "Have you seen Carise?" she demanded.

His eyes softened. "Cari." He smiled. "Pretty name."

Oh no, no, no, no, no. "Not pretty," she insisted. "My *sister*. Have you seen her?"

Jaek looked down at her arm, but the tattoo was already starting to fade. "No."

She was almost certain he was lying. He had the kind of possessive look that men got when they had pretty things they wanted to keep forever. And he wasn't allowed to have her sister.

"If you hurt her, I'll end you." It would have to be a knife in the dark, a blow he never saw coming, but she was more than capable of that.

Jaek reeled back as if she'd slapped him. "Get out! Both of you!" He shoved at Mad, and Mad stumbled before righting himself and rushing towards Jaek.

This was going to come to blows.

She forced herself to stay where she was, blocking Mad from getting in a good hit. He'd have to shove her out of the way or hit her to get to Jaek, and she knew deep down in her soul that he'd never do that.

"I think we're done here," she told Mad.

He froze where he stood, looking between her and Jaek. "Yeah, I think we are." He glared one last time at Jaek before turning and walking out.

20

MAD STRUGGLED INTERNALLY WITH THE NEXT STEP. Jadirel had eyes everywhere, so taking Kenzie back to his place was a risk. But he knew Jadirel couldn't see inside of his quarters.

In the end, it was the safest place to go, so Mad led Kenzie back there, careful to make sure they weren't being watched or followed. Soon word might go around that he was escorting a short, cloaked figure around, but hopefully everything would be over by then.

Kenzie was quiet as Mad prepared a small meal and laid it out on the table. He needed to be doing something right now or he'd scream in frustration. If he'd been offered a pit fight, he'd dive in right then and there with no weapons and come out the victor.

Instead, he poured tea for Kenzie and watched her drink it like both their lives depended on it.

"Do you think Jaek actually has Carise?" She finished the tea and set the cup down. It was the first thing she'd said to him since they'd left Jaek's cave, and it was the question that had been rattling around Mad's mind for more than an hour.

"I don't know." He sank down into the chair beside her and spread his legs just enough so his thigh brushed against hers. It was selfish and far too revealing, but it was all Mad could do to keep from scooping Kenzie in his arms and taking her back to his bed.

He should have had enough of her, should have slaked his fill. Instead, he only wanted more.

How could he convince her to take a chance on him?

"I'm going to assume he was acting out of character, right?" Her finger swirled around the edge of the teacup, the motion hypnotic.

"I don't think he's ever raised his voice at me before today, at least not outside of life-threatening situations." Jaek was a gentle giant. He'd never told Mad what landed him on Guerran, and at a certain point, Mad decided he didn't care.

"You get into a lot of life-threatening situations?" Her finger didn't pause on the rim of the cup, but Mad was almost certain Kenzie was deciding how to turn that little bit of crockery into a deadly weapon.

He shrugged. "It's Guerran."

"Right."

They ate quickly, both clearly conditioned not to let food go to waste. But Mad didn't fill his plate as high as he would have liked, instead waiting to make sure Kenzie had taken her fill first. He got a deep sense of satisfaction from watching her eat, from knowing he was taking care of her in this way.

He'd never wanted to take care of anyone on Guerran.

"You have that look on your face again," she said as she wiped her hands clean.

"What look?" Mad popped a dumpling into his mouth and savored the flavor.

"The barbarian look. Like you want to hide me away somewhere and hit anyone who gets too close with a club." She smiled when she said it.

Mad was a bit uncomfortable with how close that was to the truth. He was beginning to see the wisdom in Jaek's cave; it was much more defensible than Mad's quarters. And a club could do plenty of damage.

"I just want to feed you right now," he said calmly.

Kenzie glanced over at the bed and then back at him, but she didn't say anything.

Okay, maybe there was more he wanted to do than simply feed her, but it would all have to wait. He had to brace himself before he spoke again, knowing he was giving Kenzie a weapon that could bring him to his knees. "If Jaek has Carise, he's not holding her as a slave." He held up a hand before she could say something unconsciously—or consciously—hurtful. "He frees people from the slave market and slave ships as often as he can. He's killed more than one slaver. It goes against everything I know about the man to think he would enslave her."

"Then why wouldn't he talk about her?" Kenzie leaned back, and her hand automatically went to one of her knives, but she didn't unsheathe it. She just liked knowing that her weapons were there.

Mad wondered that himself. "Maybe he doesn't have her. Maybe he had her and she ran away."

"So he would keep her captive?" Her tone was dangerous.

He had to be careful here. If he said the wrong thing, Kenzie would march back across the city and try and get Jaek to talk at knife point. "We both know Guerran is dangerous. He wouldn't hold your sister prisoner, not exactly, but that doesn't mean he'd want her wandering around where anyone could snatch her off the street for nefarious purposes."

Kenzie sucked in a ragged breath at that image.

"The gods only know what it is. It could even be the mating urge run amok and screwing with his head." Mad only realized what he'd said when the words were out and couldn't be taken back.

Kenzie froze. "The mating urge?"

He had to back away from this conversation before it brought up uncomfortable questions. "That's very unlikely."

"Then why did you say it? What is it?" She turned toward him, their knees brushing. It was an awkward position, but she clearly wanted to watch him closely while he spoke.

"Remember what I said about fate this morning?" Explaining the mating urge felt strange. Everyone on Guerran and back home on Krudare knew the fundamentals, even if it was rare. They were taught about it as children and everyone knew the signs.

Overwhelming sexual attraction.

Ferocious possessiveness.

Intense emotion.

And something that was insufficiently called The Want.

The pull of the mating urge overrode the need

for energy from the Fount. It allowed mated pairs to freely share energy and to somehow create their own. But mostly The Want was a yawning hole inside of Mad, a hole that only Kenzie could fill by accepting their fate and tying herself to him.

"I remember," Kenzie said quietly.

Did she realize? Was she feeling even a fraction of the yearning inside of him? Could he let himself hope that *maybe* she might want him as much as he needed her?

"Some individuals are marked by fate for one another. That's what I meant by the mating urge. Fate doesn't select everyone's mate, but it happens often enough that we know it's possible." It was surreal to be speaking as if the mating urge wasn't telling him to scoop Kenzie up, place her in his bed, and never let her leave.

"You're trying to tell me soulmates are real?"

"Yes."

Kenzie shot up from her seat. "I should go."

He wanted to tell her that she could stay with him, but they both knew Jadirel could find him at any moment. "Do you have a safe place for tonight?" he asked.

She checked her weapons quickly. "I can take care of myself, Mad. I've been doing it for years. No need to worry about me."

"Maybe you shouldn't have to." It bubbled up out of him, and once he started, he couldn't stop. "Maybe you should be able to lay down your burdens for a single night. You should be cherished and protected." *Loved*. But that word he managed to claw back at the last moment. She didn't believe him when he spoke about mates. He couldn't push this yet.

"My *burdens* won't be laid down until I find my sister. And any man that wants to *cherish* me needs to know that." She looked at him in challenge.

Mad closed the distance between them and cupped her face in his hands. "We'll find her," he promised.

"I should go." She didn't step back.

Neither did Mad.

"This is crazy," she said.

Mad leaned in and kissed her.

21

Walking away was the smart thing to do. Kenzie knew that. She always did the smart thing. She *had* to do the smart thing. But the smart thing flew out of her mind the second Mad kissed her. His kiss had a way of making her burn. She'd been kissed plenty of times over the years, but it had never been like this.

All his talk about soulmates made her dream, but she had to squash that down. She didn't have time to think about the future when she had a job to do.

This kiss was in the here and now. And she could steal this time away with him; it would be enough to power her through the rest of her journey. It had to be. Because she had a feeling she was never going to get over Mad.

That was craziness. She'd known him a week. Not even a week! And yet he'd already carved a place in her heart that was his for good. He'd left his mark on her.

And she wanted more.

Kenzie wrapped her legs around his hips, giving him all her weight and trusting him to hold her up. He did it like she weighed nothing. And the angle of the kiss got even better. He was too tall, really. Or he should have been. But they were both determined to make it work.

His tongue cast a spell on her, and she gladly gave into his magic. She loved the feel of his hair through her fingers, and she moaned as one of his hands cupped her ass. There were too many clothes between them, but if she wanted him naked, she'd have to let him go.

She wanted to keep enjoying this for as long as she could.

They'd fucked that morning. It should have been enough. He should have been out of her system by now. She'd never felt this kind of need for anyone before.

How was she supposed to cope?

More kissing. Definitely more kissing.

She wanted him to give into his most barbaric urges and rip her clothes off of her, but some tiny bit of sanity intruded to remind her that she didn't exactly have a huge wardrobe and she couldn't afford to lose more garments.

But she could imagine the feel of him tearing through her clothes and throwing her on the bed, looming over her and taking her like some kind of warrior king of old.

Fuck. Yes.

Someday.

If they had someday.

She wanted someday more than she knew how.

Mad laid her on the bed and pulled away despite the way she clung to him. She would have been embarrassed by the sound that came out of her mouth if it hadn't made his eyes darken in desire.

She reached for her buttons, but Mad grabbed her wrists and wrenched them up above her head before undoing the buttons himself.

He wanted to play it like that? Okay. Kenzie could play along. But if he wanted to keep her in place, he was going to have to use that wonderful strength of his.

Or his lips. Fuck, yes, those were good too.

He bared her breasts to the cool air of the room, but that wasn't what made her nipples harden. No, that was the lust surging through her and making her wanton. He leaned down and used that marvelous tongue of his, sucking on her tits and making her moan even louder.

Kenzie didn't care if his neighbors could hear. All she cared about right then was him and the sensations he gave her.

How did it get better each time they came together?

What would it be like if they *kept* doing this?

She didn't think her mind could handle it. Mad worshiped her breasts like she was laid out on an altar, and she'd never felt more like a sensual goddess. Her body was on fire, and she was so wet she was practically dripping. She could feel his cock brush against her, but he seemed content to ignore it.

For now.

She wanted him inside of her. She was empty and she needed him. And with every tease of his tongue, he brought her closer and closer to the edge without even touching her cunt.

Yet.

He kissed his way down and hiked the skirt of her tunic up until she was bared to him, legs spread and ready for more. Mad was clearly determined to drive her crazy with want, and Kenzie was happy to go along for the ride.

His tongue found her cunt, and all she could do

was writhe under him as he did wicked things to her. Writhe under him and beg for more. The man was a master and she his willing instrument. The sounds he coaxed from her were notes she didn't know she could hit.

And still he demanded more.

Her barbarian was relentless. She was his spoils and would have been more than happy to be conquered. But she'd jumped in his bed herself.

She'd be crazy to ever leave.

Reality tried to intrude, and Kenzie shoved it aside. For now, she had Mad and she would enjoy it. Dwelling on the future only led to hurt and worry. She didn't need that, not right now.

Mad slid a finger into her wet entrance, and Kenzie gasped. The gasp turned into a groan as a second finger joined. She was more than ready for his cock, but the man was determined to make this last.

She couldn't complain.

Her fingers clutched at the edge of his bed, digging into the mattress so she didn't reach down and try to take control. This was his show and she was loving it. She could take over later.

Maybe.

But why would she want to when he was determined to make her brain melt with pleasure?

She danced on the edge of orgasm for so long that she knew she had to be begging him to let her come, but her words weren't quite coherent. And from the satisfied smirk Mad gave her, that was exactly what he wanted.

Then he went back to work, and she couldn't stop the orgasm if she tried. It ripped through her and she called out his name, hips bucking against him as her body rippled.

How did he make her feel so much? How could he give her even more?

She was still breathing hard as Mad covered her body, holding himself over her like he was doing a push up. He grinned down at her, looking very proud of himself. "Can you take me?" he asked.

Asked? More like challenged. And Kenzie was ready for more. "Try me."

Mad groaned and kissed her roughly. Kenzie loved it. His control was on the edge, and she wanted him to let go. She wanted to see what happened when the barbarian inside was unleashed.

And as he thrust inside of her, that was it. This was no slow lovemaking. Mad took her with a groan, hips moving quickly and setting a pace she could barely match. But Kenzie wanted everything he could give her, and match it she did.

He held her tight enough to leave bruises, and she loved the thought of wearing his mark. She wanted this man branded under her skin where she could never forget him.

Her body surrendered again, shuddering around him in ecstasy, and Mad followed quickly after.

They lay together as they came down from their passion, and Kenzie wished she could stay. Sleep clawed at her and it would be so easy to give into it, to let Mad gather her close and hold her through the night.

She wanted it more than she wanted almost anything.

But people were looking for her, and she'd almost been discovered at Mad's place once before.

"Don't go yet," Mad said into the darkness around them. "Stay just a bit longer."

Not the night. He knew she couldn't do that, and she was grateful he didn't ask. If he had, she wasn't sure she could make herself say no.

"Just a few more minutes," she agreed. She let him hold her, but she fought off sleep with every mental weapon she had. She couldn't give in. Not tonight.

What would it be to spend a night with this man for real? The first time didn't count, not when it had ended with her knife at his throat.

This thing between them was dangerously real. And that scared Kenzie enough to finally sneak out of bed. Mad teetered on the edge of sleep and only made a mumbling noise of protest.

She looked back at him one last time after she was dressed and almost leaned in to kiss him. But if she kissed him, she knew she wouldn't leave.

She forced herself to climb out his window without looking back.

But she knew she'd left a piece of her heart in that bed with him.

22

Something woke Mad up. He was alone in his bed, and it had never felt more empty. He knew Kenzie couldn't stay, not when Jadirel was desperate to get his hands on her, but that didn't mean he didn't crave her company.

Soon, he promised himself. Soon he'd find a way to be by her side.

Even if it meant leaving Guerran.

Could he really? For so long he'd struggled on this hopeless planet, hoping that one day he might be reunited with his sister. But there were tens of thousands of exiles on Guerran. How many had been pardoned over the years? A hundred? The chance of actually getting a pardon was minuscule.

If he left with Kenzie, he could have a life. If she would have him.

Mad heard another noise.

He stayed still in his bed. There was a knife on the bedside table and his axe was right under the bed, but he didn't want any intruder to know he was awake until it was too late. His fists could do plenty of damage before he had to reach for a weapon.

Heavy footsteps tromped through the room and threw open the door to his bathing chamber. Whoever was here wasn't trying to hide.

Mad sat up and reached for his knife. He didn't turn on the light, it would make his quarters a beacon for anyone looking in from the outside. The moonlight streaming in provided enough illumination to make out his intruder.

Jaek.

He spun around as if he'd heard Mad sit up. "She's gone. Where is she?" He turned back toward the bathing chamber, dove in, and then came right back out once he'd assessed it was empty.

"I'm the only one here." Mad put the knife back down with a fair bit of reluctance. Jaek looked ready to brawl, and Mad might need to defend himself, but he wasn't about to stab his friend.

Jaek growled again and slammed his fist against the wall. The room shook.

Okay. Mad slid out of bed and made for the

kitchen. They needed to talk. He had alcohol, but he had a feeling they were both going to need clear heads. Tea it was, then.

"Are you saying you had Carise at some point?" Kenzie would be enraged that they'd been so close to her sister and let her go.

"Cari's gone. Jadirel's men." He sank down onto one of the chairs and accepted his drink.

"Then why did you come here looking for her?" Mad supposed he *was* one of Jadirel's men, but both he and Jaek knew the truth of that.

"Looking for the other one." Jaek scowled, eyes scanning the room as if Kenzie would magically appear.

"I'm not sure where Kenzie is right now. We're meeting up again tomorrow. But I need to understand what happened. Why didn't you tell us you had Carise?" Mad had a few guesses. He'd never seen Jaek like this before, and there wasn't much that could drive a man to this state.

"She's *mine*," Jaek ground out, every syllable daring Mad to contradict him. "Not letting her go."

"She's your mate?" Kenzie wasn't going to like that one bit.

Jaek didn't confirm it. "I have to get her back."

"Calm down. Drink your tea." He'd turned into

the nanny who had raised him and Taiana, always pushing tea on everyone. Another reminder of the home he'd never see again.

Jaek drank his tea.

"How long has Carise been with you? Are you bonded? Does she know about the connection? Does she trust you?" Kenzie was going to be angry and confused when she learned about this, and Mad had to manage things before everything exploded in his face.

"She trusts me," Jaek said. He didn't answer any of the other questions.

Mad put that aside for now. "When was she taken?"

"A few hours ago." The teacup looked tiny in Jaek's hands, and Mad was half sure the man would crush it in his frustration.

"Do you know who took her?" It wasn't Jadirel, clearly. He didn't do his own dirty work.

"Baryn and that new kid he has working for him. Gav. I have security footage of them dragging her away." His eyes grew desperate. "She was struggling. She tried to fight. Baryn slapped her. I'll kill him."

Kenzie was going to be even angrier when she learned the man she'd spared had harmed her sister. "You may need to get in line."

That confounded Jaek for a moment. "What?"

"Kenzie beat Baryn in the pit but didn't kill him." Mad couldn't wipe the small smile off his face at the memory. She was an artist with her weapons.

"Impossible. Cari said—" He cut himself off.

So they'd discussed Kenzie. It was only fair. He felt like he knew Carise. But Kenzie had changed a lot since the last time her little sister had seen her. What about Carise?

"I saw the fight with my own eyes."

Jaek stood up.

"Where are you going?" Mad needed him here now, needed to figure out a plan of attack before Jaek did something stupid.

"To find Cari."

And there it was. Mad glared. "Sit your ass back down. We're going to get her back. I promise. But that's not going to happen if you rush into Jadirel's palace without any backup. Now tell me, are you *sure* Baryn and Gav were working for Jadirel?"

Jaek nodded swiftly, still glaring as if Mad was wasting his time.

This was not going to be an easy conversation, and Mad definitely hadn't caught enough sleep to deal with it. Too bad. "Okay. I have a way into Jadirel's palace. We're going to get Carise back. You have my word."

"How?"

Mad wished he knew.

23

ANXIETY THRUMMED THROUGH KENZIE AS SHE MADE HER way to where she was supposed to meet up with Mad. She'd tossed and turned all night in her blankets and could not be further from rested. Which was stupid. She'd spent most of her life sleeping alone. She couldn't remember the last time she'd taken a man to her bed. One night in Mad's arms shouldn't have made it impossible to walk away.

And yet it had been harder to walk away from him the night before than it should have been.

Soulmates are real.

And that was a thought she couldn't shake. It didn't matter. It *couldn't* matter. And yet she'd spent half the night wondering if... nope. She wasn't going there. That way lay dragons, and she didn't want to get eaten by the specter of hope.

She had to focus on the mission. Carise was still on Guerran, she was sure of it. She was going to find her sister and... then what?

Would Carise want to go back to Earth? Would she ever feel safe enough there after her abduction? Was there even a life for them back on Earth? Kenzie hadn't heard from their father once since she left. He had a way to contact her; she'd made sure to leave him with that lifeline. But he'd never used it.

Would he care if they came back?

Was he even still alive?

That question should have been a knife to the chest. Instead, she felt a tiny pang and nothing more. If their father was dead, that was truly the last tie they had left to Earth. If he wasn't... well, he hadn't exactly ever been Father of the Year.

She'd do whatever Carise wanted.

But what do you *want?* The voice in her head sounded suspiciously like Mad. And since he wasn't actually standing next to her, she couldn't tell him to shut up. She didn't have the luxury of wanting things when she had to find Carise.

She wanted Mad.

Luxury or no, that desire couldn't be denied. And if Kenzie was honest with herself, she wasn't trying too hard. She kept falling into his bed, and it got harder and harder to crawl out of it.

Would she manage it next time? She wasn't fooling herself into thinking there wouldn't be a next time.

Would he come with her and Carise when it was time to leave?

The thought nearly knocked her over. Yes, she was attracted to Mad. But she'd known him less than a week. She couldn't ask him to leave his entire life behind and give up any hope of ever seeing *his* sister again just for some good —great—sex.

Soulmates are real.

She had to stop thinking about that. Mad hadn't been talking about them. And there was no way Jaek was actually Carise's soulmate. Carise was still basically a kid. She was too young for a soulmate.

A little voice reminded Kenzie that Carise was twenty-four now. A little older than Kenzie had been when she took off for her stint on EarthCol3. If Kenzie had been old enough to make her own decisions, wasn't Carise?

That was a problem for *after* she got her sister back.

When she made it to the meeting spot, her worries were pushed to the back of her mind. Mad was already there, and he looked like crap.

"Have you slept?" She was already close to him,

a hand on his shoulder and breathing in his mascu-line scent.

How did the man smell so damn good?

He gave her a faint smile and a short kiss that made her heart flip. It was so... casual, as if they'd been kissing for years and would keep doing it forever. And it was scary how much she wanted that.

"I caught an hour or so. Maybe two." He was dressed for war today, his leathers all in place and his axe slung over his back.

"What happened?" Kenzie never should have left his quarters. If he'd been attacked, she could back him up. If something else had happened, she could comfort him.

Mad stepped away from her and braced himself as if he knew she wouldn't like what he had to say next. "Jaek came to me a little while after you left. Carise was staying with him, but she was taken by two men working for Jadirel: Baryn and Gav."

"The same Baryn whose ass I kicked in the pit?"

He nodded.

And then the rest of what he said caught up. "Jaek had Carise? We were *that* close? If we hadn't walked away, she would be with me right now. How did he lose her? Where is she? Why didn't you get me the second you heard?" She realized her hand was on her knife only as she started to pull it out, and she forced herself to let go. She wasn't going to stab Mad, not when he knew where Carise was.

He had his hands up to placate her. "He came for help when he could. I didn't know where you were sleeping, and I wasn't going to risk leading Jadirel's men to *you* when there was nothing we could do until morning anyway. He's had her for a few hours, and I know that's bad. But we know where your sister is. We're going to get her back."

She needed to stab something. Someone. She needed to *move*. She knew Carise had been through hell in the last few years, but this was different. Kenzie had met Jadirel. She'd seen the way he treated humans. "If he's put a collar around her throat, I'm going to gut him. Slowly." And she'd enjoy it. She didn't like violence, no matter how good she was at it. But she'd use every trick she'd learned in the last seven years to cause him as much pain as a person could feel before she ended his sorry existence.

"You said you'd go through hell to find your sister. Did you mean it?"

"Of course I meant it." She could list off all the terrible things she'd seen in the past two years, but they didn't have time, and she was tired of standing around. "Whatever the plan is, yes, I'm in. She's less than two miles away from me when we've been light-years apart for nearly a decade. I want her back today."

Mad nodded solemnly. He opened his mouth, but closed it again before he could make a noise. If he had something more to say, he'd decided not to share it. "Jadirel tasked me with returning you to him. It's the only way I can think to get close enough to challenge him without needing to strip out of my weapons. Will you let me take you to him?"

She was a fool to consider it. Mad could be playing a game right now. She'd been betrayed by contacts before. And if she judged him wrong, *she'd* be the one in a collar by the end of the day.

But he was leading her to her sister. He didn't need to lie. He could have turned her over to Jadirel at any point. And she trusted him, simple as that. Maybe that made her reckless, but at some point, she needed to trust someone.

Mad wouldn't betray her.

Soulmates are real.

She didn't know if he was hers, but the belief that he could be was enough to propel her forward. She could trust Mad. He knew why she was here and what she needed. And right now, they needed to work together to finish her mission.

"Let's go get my sister back."

24

Kenzie tripped over her feet, and her cheeks burned at the humiliation. The chains on her hands clinked, and she could feel the eyes of everyone in Jadirel's territory on her as Mad dragged her through the street.

It's for Carise, she reminded herself. Again.

Jadirel had Carise. This was the only way to get close enough to get her back. She trusted Mad for some crazy reason, and she really hoped she hadn't judged poorly.

The walls and stained glass windows of Jadirel's palace mocked her as Mad stopped at the entrance and spoke to the guards.

"You finally found her," one of them chuckled darkly, looking at her in a way that had her reaching for her knives.

Except she was unarmed.

If Mad betrayed her, she was going to *kill* him.

"She's not for you." Mad scowled, but didn't sound possessive. He sounded *bored*. "Jadirel wants her, and I'm going to deliver her. No one else is getting the credit for this."

The guard blew out a breath and glared at Mad. But he let them pass.

Mad was fully decked out in his best warrior gear, leathers in place, axe on his back, and a knife on his hip. She'd even let him borrow her baton just in case he needed another weapon. He was the size of a supersoldier, and she had to believe that he would be strong enough to defeat Jadirel himself.

Otherwise, she was dead.

Kenzie wouldn't let Jadirel put a collar on her. She would die fighting. And she had to mentally apologize to Carise for her weakness, but she couldn't *let* herself be taken. It wasn't in her.

A stronger woman would be willing to live through anything.

They entered the narrow passage that led to Jadirel's throne room. This was their last chance to be alone. Possibly forever.

Kenzie wanted to launch herself at Mad and kiss the living daylights out of him. Dread hung over her like a curse, and she couldn't help but fear that Jadirel was too strong. She'd never seen the exile king fight, but he'd hung onto his power here for years.

There could be eyes on them right now, but Kenzie risked taking a step forward. Mad whipped around and clasped her forearm. To anyone else, it might have looked like he was stopping her from hitting him.

Instead, it was as close to an embrace as they could manage.

Their eyes locked, and Kenzie could feel Mad's gaze all the way down to her soul. And something that had been tickling the back of Kenzie's mind finally annoyed her enough that she had to speak.

Mad had been protecting her this entire time, even when it was clear that she could handle herself. And when he'd talked about mates, there was something missing. "I think you're holding something back from me," she spoke, barely above a whisper, just in case there were hidden guards or recording devices. "When you were talking about fate. And mates. And the future. I know we don't have time for you to explain, but whatever it is, I want you to do whatever you need to get us to the other side of this thing. No matter what."

Mad's face went a bit pale. "You don't know

what you're saying." She couldn't tell if his voice trembled with fear or hope.

She wanted it to be hope. Under other circumstances, she would have covered her hand with his as a sign of trust, but she was still bound. So she had to use her words. "I trust you." She wouldn't have let anyone else put her in chains.

They stood like that for an eternity, but it must have really only been a few seconds. Not long after that, there was a knock against the door leading into Jadirel's throne room ,and Mad dragged her inside.

The two humans were chained beside the throne, and Kenzie didn't have to try to hide her disgust this time. Two other Kru'dari, a man and a woman, stood to one side of Jadirel's throne.

The spectacle would have witnesses.

Mad stilled in front of her, and Kenzie knew something was wrong. The door shut behind them, locking them in with Jadirel. She stepped to the side as best as she could and saw that Jadirel was wearing a strange glowing necklace today.

She'd seen that before. On the guard in the green zone. They were important, but she couldn't remember what they were called.

Jadirel stroked a finger along the leather pouch and grinned. "I was lucky enough to get a nearly full

Pitcher. I can't remember the last time that happened. Now bring the girl forward."

Pitcher. It took a second, and then Kenzie remembered. The pouches contained energy from Krudare, energy that could make them stronger, faster, and more resilient fighters.

This was bad. Really, really bad.

"Anything," Kenzie whispered to Mad. If he had a trick up his sleeve, she needed him to pull it.

Immediately.

A headache started to form at the back of her skull, and Kenzie took a deep breath. Mad was going to win. He had to.

The headache got worse.

"I don't have all day, Damari," Jadirel jeered.

Mad pulled out a knife and threw it straight at Jadirel's face.

25

ON A NORMAL DAY, MAD WOULD HAVE TROUBLE defeating Jadirel. He was bigger and faster than the exile king, but Jadirel was mean, tricky, and more experienced. He'd been a star in the pit during his rise to power, and Mad had never faced him one on one.

With a Pitcher, Jadirel would be nearly unstoppable.

The mating bond rose in Mad, and he thrust it out toward Kenzie, needing to tie her to him. The energy their lovemaking had given him was strong, but already beginning to fade. If they were fully bound, he would be nearly as strong as he was back on Krudare.

Maybe even stronger than Jadirel.

But he met a brick wall of resistance in Kenzie.

She might have given him permission, but she didn't know what he needed. Physical contact could do the trick, but Jadirel was already coming at him. Mad dropped Kenzie's chain and hoped she was smart enough to step back.

"This is a challenge," he declared, just in case Jadirel's people tried to contest it later or interfere. There weren't exactly laws on Guerran, but there were customs, and once a challenge was started, it was until the death or submission.

Mad couldn't submit.

He heard metal fall to the ground and knew Kenzie had undone the chains around her hands. He hadn't been willing to fully bind her, and though she'd been willing, he'd seen the relief when he showed her the trick to undo the chain.

The energy in Jadirel's Pitcher teased Mad, but there was no way to take it for himself now that it had been keyed to Jadirel, not without killing the man, which was already the plan.

"You're a fool," Jadirel scowled, holding a thick metal chain and twirling it around before whipping it out towards Mad. The man didn't like blades for some reason. "You've thrown your life away."

Mad didn't respond. Talking would tire him out faster, and he had to conserve his energy. He tried the mating bond again, but Kenzie still resisted. Was there a way to explain what he needed? He didn't have the words.

He pulled out his axe in a swift move and swung at Jadirel, even though he had little hope of connecting. The axe was a weapon of fear, and he saw the way the exile king flinched.

Good.

If Mad was going to die today, he wanted Jadirel to know fear. But Mad couldn't die. Not when he was all that was standing between Kenzie and Jadirel's collar.

Jadirel swung his chain again and it swiped against Mad's side, dull pain blooming in his muscles. That chain was going to hurt if he got hit somewhere important. Or if Jadirel kept connecting.

Mad swiped out with his axe again and felt a keen sense of satisfaction as the edge kissed Jadirel's skin.

First blood.

But the Pitcher around Jadirel's neck glowed even brighter, and the nick sealed itself like it had never been there.

Stupid waste of power.

But it was an unwelcome reminder that Jadirel had power to spare.

Mad was constantly trying to connect to Kenzie with the mating bond now, and when he spun to avoid a hit from Jadirel, he saw her eyes drawn together in pain. He tried to reach out and touch her, to cinch the bond between them, but Jadirel's chain wrapped around his arm and he was pulled further away.

Rather than try and untangle it, Mad grabbed onto the chain and dragged Jadirel close. At this range, his axe was useless and he dropped it, going instead for the baton Kenzie had given him.

He struck out with it, making Jadirel groan in pain as blood bloomed on his face, but the man didn't go down. He wouldn't until the power of his Pitcher was exhausted. That would take hours if Jadirel kept wasting his power to heal minor wounds, days if he stopped bothering.

Mad had to take him out with one blow, fast and deadly enough that the Pitcher couldn't heal him.

He whacked Jadirel again, but the exile king still had control of the chain. Mad stumbled and fell.

Kenzie gasped.

Time narrowed into a thin sliver, and Mad watched in slow motion as Jadirel came down on him, an evil smile on his face and death in his eyes. Mad rolled out of the way, but still felt the blow of Jadirel's fist against him.

He was tangled up in the chain, unable to get up. He managed to get one hand free and reached for the Pitcher at Jadirel's throat, tearing it off with a vicious tug and throwing it across the room. Jadirel was still connected to it, but it would be harder to draw on the energy now.

Mad kicked up and scurried back, freeing himself while Jadirel howled in distraction and looked around for the Pitcher. He got untangled from the chain, but Jadirel was already back and ready to fight, the Pitcher forgotten and Mad's axe in his hands.

The bastard.

Mad exchanged the baton for a knife. He was going to gut the exile king until there was nothing left inside of him.

Jadirel swung, and it would have connected if Mad didn't jump a foot back. That was a killing blow, and Jadirel was still fucking strong.

But he couldn't be cautious. Mad rushed Jadirel, blade out and ready. But his blade glanced against Jadirel's leathers and didn't do any damage. He switched tactics, punching at Jadirel's kidney and taking deep satisfaction when the man grunted.

He couldn't find a weak spot to stab, but his punches were doing damage. Mad regretted letting the axe go. *That* would have cleaved through leather armor without issue.

Jadirel figured out the axe wasn't made for close

quarters and dropped it. Then he used the tricks he was famous for, stomping on Mad's foot, following it up with a knee to the groin, and finishing with a blow to Mad's head.

Mad didn't stand a chance, and it was his own damn fault. He fell to the floor, trying to breathe through the pain and get away, but Jadirel gave no mercy, kicking him in the stomach and taking his time in doling out the punishment.

"You insolent whelp," Jadirel spat. "I'm going to make you hurt before you die. And then I'll put your head on a pike." He kicked again, and Mad was almost certain one of his ribs snapped.

He looked over and saw Kenzie standing there, and he reached out with the mate bond one desperate, final time.

Her eyes widened, and she must have realized what he wanted. The bond between them snapped into place and energy rushed into Mad. The pain faded to almost nothing as adrenaline sizzled in his veins.

His fingers brushed against his axe and he grabbed it. And as Jadirel prepared for another kick, Mad surged up, swinging with all his might and cleaving into Jadirel.

The exile king screamed as he toppled to the floor, but the sound faded to almost nothing in a moment as blood gushed out of him and his life poured out around them. Out of the corner of his eye, Mad saw the forgotten Pitcher blaze with energy, but it wasn't enough to undo Mad's damage.

Jadirel was dead. Mad was the exile king.

Kenzie screamed.

26

Kenzie felt the blade of a knife whisper against her throat a moment before her instincts kicked in. She screamed, more to distract her attacker than out of fear, and struck at his hand, clearing the knife from her throat and giving her space to maneuver.

She stomped on his foot and twisted her body, locking the Kru'dari's arm and grabbing the knife as it fell, holding it to his side where it could sink in and nick his liver in no time.

By the time Mad looked over at her, it was done.

He looked... different. By killing Jadirel he'd taken the man's place. He was the exile king now, and power emanated from him. But that wasn't it.

He looked fucking hot. But Kenzie couldn't get distracted when she was holding a struggling warrior. One wrong move and he'd turn the tables right back on her. Yeah, not going to happen.

Mad strode forward and grabbed the Kru'dari by the throat, slamming him down to the ground. "You *dare* to put your hands on my mate!"

Mate. Right. Oh. So that was the weird connection she could feel snap into place while Mad had been lying there on the brink of death. It had been almost impossible to focus on the fight with the pounding in her head, but the moment she stopped trying to fight the headache, it had disappeared, and a strange connection was left in its place.

If she closed her eyes, she could still feel Mad. She'd know where he was, and his emotions swam around with hers. Right now, he was riding high on the rush of victory and the anger that this man had touched her.

She wondered what else they could do. She knew he was taking energy from her, but she didn't feel any weaker. If anything, she was exhilarated. It was as if whatever was between them was causing the energy that lived inside of her to multiply. This wasn't whatever sick bond Jadirel had forced on his prisoners.

This was something beautiful.

But the look on Mad's face was anything but at the moment. He towered over the Kru'dari and looked ready to take up the mantle of executioner. She didn't care if he killed the Kru'dari. The man had willingly worked for Jadirel.

Then again, so had Mad.

Kenzie walked up to Mad and placed a hand on his shoulder. "Back off, big guy. You want to think it through before you make your first execution."

Mad was frozen over the man for several moments before he let go and stepped back, grabbing Kenzie's hand and tugging her along with him. The man on the floor held perfectly still, as if he was hoping Mad couldn't see him if he didn't move.

"Get out of my territory," Mad growled at him. "I won't be nice if I see you again."

The man ran, and his flight notified the guards at the door that something was wrong. They came running in and four more came from different hallways. They looked at Mad and then looked at Jadirel's body on the floor.

"I witnessed it," the Kru'dari woman beside Jadirel's—Mad's—throne said. "It was a fair challenge."

As one, all six guards bowed to Mad. Mad glared at them and held on tighter to her. It was only then that Kenzie realized how nervous he really was. She knew he didn't want to be an exile king, but he'd just taken on this role.

For her.

"Carise," she whispered. Her sister had to be close. She didn't know what she would do if they'd done all this work for her to be gone. "And the two beside the throne."

Mad gave a slight nod and addressed the head guard. "Unchain these two. If they want to leave, give them credits." He turned to the humans, who both had carefully blank expressions on their faces. His voice softened. "You are welcome to stay for now. I can have rooms made up for you. You're not prisoners anymore. Your choice." Then he turned back to the guards. "Give each of them no less than what they were purchased for, plus monthly wages for every month they were held."

One of the guards opened his mouth, and Mad glared at him. Kenzie probably shouldn't have found it so hot. But the man sure as hell knew how to command a room.

And he was all hers.

"I want to know how many other people Jadirel enslaved. I won't imprison them another night."

One of the guards rushed forward to the woman prisoner and unlocked her collar with shaking hands before moving on to the male. The woman surged forward and one of the guards yelled, but Kenzie stepped between the woman and the guards before the guards could do anything stupid.

The woman towered over Jadirel's body and kicked him in the stomach with all her might. It would have hurt... if he'd been alive. When she put her foot down, she slipped in his blood, and Kenzie held an arm out to steady her.

The woman's eyes were wild, and Kenzie thought she would run. There was nothing to say to her that would make things better. Kenzie said nothing at all. The woman looked back down at Jadirel and spat.

Then she looked over at Mad. "I want a shower. And clothing." She made the demands like she was asking for a pile of gold.

Mad nodded. He looked to the nearest guard. "See it done. And if you are inappropriate with her, the punishment will be severe."

Kenzie never thought she'd see a seven-foot-tall alien cower, but it was a day of firsts. "Carise," she said again. She was getting anxious. What if someone had taken her already? What if she was in trouble again?

"There was another human brought here," said Mad. This time he looked at the woman who had witnessed his challenge. "She looks a lot like my mate. Her name is Carise. I want her brought to me."

Then he turned to the guards. "And I want this mess cleaned up."

"We can send for servants," said one of the braver guards.

Mad started to nod, then paused. "Are those servants paid?"

The head guard nodded quickly. "Yes, sire. The only slaves are the ones Ki—that is, the ones Jadirel kept for himself."

"Very well. Have this place cleaned. And bring Carise to us in the antechamber." He led Kenzie through the guards into a side room she hadn't noticed before.

Once the door closed behind them, he slumped against it, most of the bravado going out of him. Kenzie wrapped her arms around him and let herself fall into the hug. He was huge and comforting, even if she was supposed to be the one comforting him.

"I'll have them make up a nice room for Carise. I don't know where she was forced to sleep before. But it will have a big bed and a window. You've found her." Mad was making promises, but he didn't move from where they were holding each other.

Kenzie was supposed to feel happy. And she was. Distantly. But sheer relief had flooded out everything else. After two years, she was about to be reunited with her sister once more. She could barely believe that this day had come.

But what did that mean for her and Mad?

He'd just taken power of a territory on Guerran for her. He was a king. And maybe one day he could get a pardon and go home. She was about to take Carise and get as far away from Guerran as a person could.

And yet Mad was her mate. How could she leave him behind?

How could she ask him to go with her?

There was a knock on the door, and she stepped back from Mad.

He offered her a grin. "She's here."

27

Mad ducked out of the antechamber when Carise was brought in, and as soon as Kenzie saw her sister, she forgot about everything else.

Carise was alive! She was here!

Kenzie launched herself at her baby sister and clamped her arms around her, tears falling down her face in rivulets as the full reality of the situation settled over her. Carise hugged her back so tightly that Kenzie had trouble breathing. She didn't care. Air was overrated.

They were alone in the antechamber, and Kenzie made sure the door was closed. She wanted privacy. If she and her sister could stay alone in this room for the next year, it wouldn't be enough.

The hug went on for a long time, but eventually they separated, and Kenzie ushered her sister back to a small couch that was pushed up against the wall. Now that she had time to look around the room, she realized it was more like a sitting room than an office.

There were shelves of books, a couch, two chairs, and a low table. All the comforts a busy king needed. The room was decorated in lush, warm colors, and there was a painting on one wall of a verdant scene that looked nothing like what she'd seen of Guerran. Was that Krudare?

She didn't care. Carise was right next to her.

But now that she had her sister, words got caught in her throat. There were shadows in Carise's eyes, evidence of horrors she'd endured at the hands of who knows how many tormentors. And Kenzie wouldn't ask about it. Not today. Today she was just going to be happy that she had her sister safe and sound.

"You're taller!" It was inane, but true. When she'd left Earth for her stint on EarthCol3, Carise had been an inch shorter than her. Now she was an inch taller than her, and Kenzie was pretty sure she hadn't shrunk.

Carise smiled faintly. "It happened after Earth. Space supplements or something."

Right. Kenzie let *that* drop. She didn't want to open up old wounds. "How long have you been on

Guerran?" She needed to know how far behind she was, even if she had a pretty tight timeline of this planet.

Carise relaxed a little against the couch and pulled her legs up, looping an arm around them. There were scars on that arm, and Kenzie tried not to stare. She probably failed. Did Carise want to go on a vengeance spree? Because that could easily be arranged.

"About a month, I think." Her voice was raspy. It hadn't been raspy before.

Kenzie didn't ask. Not yet. She was going to choke on all the questions she wasn't asking. But there was one she couldn't resist. "What's up with Jaek?"

Carise brightened, and it was like she had her sister back. But just for a second. Her expression closed off, and she looked to the side, away from Kenzie. "He was nice. He kept me safe."

What was that even supposed to mean? Kenzie wanted to push. She wanted Carise to account for every second since they'd last seen one another more than two years ago. But Carise looked tired, and Kenzie was so happy to have her sister back that she didn't want to dwell on the bad stuff.

"He's... um... big." And though Carise was now frustratingly one inch taller than her, she was still small. She'd lost weight and was edging towards frail rather than thin.

Really, a vengeance quest was starting to sound nice.

Kenzie kept the bloodthirstiness to herself.

Carise blushed and hid her face behind her knees. "They're all big here. How did you do this? How are you here? Am I dreaming?"

Kenzie wanted to cry. Whoever had taken her sister deserved to be banished to the deepest pit of hell. Carise was a sweet soul, and back home she'd never hurt a fly. "I'm really here," Kenzie assured her, reaching out and clutching her hand to anchor her in the moment. "I made a lot of contact back on EarthCol3, and I called in every favor. I haven't stopped looking since I found out you were gone. Then I got here and I found you."

Carise didn't need to know about the blood Kenzie had spilled, the darkness she'd endured to find Carise. That was Kenzie's burden to bear.

"It shouldn't be too difficult to get passage off of Guerran," Kenzie assured her, even as her heart broke in half at the thought of leaving Mad behind. She had to think about Carise now. That was the mission, it had always been the plan. "We're a long way from Earth. But we can probably be home for Christmas. I think. I'm not actually sure what month it is back home. But if we missed it, we can have our own."

"Don't tell me you're going to make fruitcake," Carise moaned, her face a mass of exaggerated horror.

"I will make fruitcake and you're going to like it. No matter how burned it is." Kenzie had forgotten about her baking experiments back when she'd been a teenager. They hadn't gone well, and she could taste the phantom flavor of burnt flour on her tongue. "Or we could do cookies. Ham. Mashed potatoes. Mac and cheese. Whatever you want, we'll have."

"What—" Carise cut herself off.

"We don't have to do Christmas," Kenzie was quick to say. "Right, what am I thinking. If I had found you sooner—"

"What? No!" Carise interrupted. "You crossed the galaxy to find me, that's practically impossible. And you did it in two years!" Now it was Carise's turn to grip Kenzie's hands.

But Kenzie couldn't take her absolution. "You should have never been taken in the first place. If I hadn't abandoned you at home, you would have been safe. And when we get back, you don't have to worry. No matter what. You're not getting taken again."

Carise was quiet for a moment, and then she smiled. "I would like ham. And pie."

"Consider it done."

They talked for an hour or more before Mad came in and let them know Carise had a room made up for the night.

"You should sleep," Kenzie told her as they followed a servant down the winding hallways to the room Carise had been assigned. The room was nice with a huge bed, a window overlooking the city, and a fire blazing in the fireplace.

"I'm not tired," Carise insisted, even as she sat on the bed.

"Food then?" Kenzie wasn't sure when she'd last eaten.

Carise nodded.

Kenzie summoned the servant back and put in the order, and in a matter of minutes, they each had a glass of wine and a plate laden with meats, cheese, and fruit. "No pie. Sorry."

Carise sipped her wine and rolled her eyes. "You don't have to keep apologizing for everything. It's not your fault. I can wait for my goddamn pie."

The outburst was a bit shocking, but Kenzie did her best to keep smiling. Of course Carise would have outbursts. She'd been through a big trauma. "Drink up," she just said.

They ate their way through the meal, and eventually Carise yawned. It didn't take her long before she was curled up on the bed and sleeping.

Kenzie watched her sister's chest rise and fall in an even rhythm and didn't stop the tears that started to stream down her face. Every emotion was mixed up inside of her: happiness, relief, sorrow, confusion.

Her mission was over. She'd found her sister.

So what the hell was she supposed to do now?

28

Kenzie couldn't watch Carise sleep all night, no matter how much she wanted to. For one, it was barely night. Secondly, she had a feeling Mad was going to need her. And if she was about to say goodbye to her mate forever, she wanted to spend as many seconds with him as she could.

Mad was alone in the throne room when she walked in. He slouched on the throne like a king in repose. Put a crown on his head and he'd fit right in. But he was a man made for the axe he slung across his back, not a crown.

"I thought you'd still be with your sister," he said. Mad looked around for some reason and then stood. "You need a place to sit."

"I've been sitting all day. You did the hard part.

And Carise is asleep. I had the servant put a dose of melatonin in her wine."

Mad reared back. "You *drugged* her?"

"It's melatonin. It just helps you sleep. It's not really a sedative. After all this shit, she deserves a good sleep." Kenzie crossed her arms and glared at Mad. This could be their last hour together, and he was going to argue with her?

"I don't think she'd like that."

"What am I supposed to do?" It burst out of her, and the tears threatened to fall again, but she wasn't sure she had any left. She'd cried for a long, *long* time in Carise's room. "She's been through fucking hell for the past two years. I just want to bundle her up and find somewhere safe to keep her forever. And I don't want her to have to think about all the shit that's happened. So, yes, I gave her a small dose of melatonin to help her sleep. I'm sorry if that makes me a monster. She needed rest. You didn't see how tired she looked."

Masculine arms clamped around her, and Kenzie surrendered to Mad's embrace. *This* was where she belonged, and she clung to him, knowing she'd have to soak up enough of these moments to last the rest of her life.

"I'll apologize in the morning," she muttered.

She shouldn't have done it, and it shouldn't have taken Mad yelling at her to realize that. Carise was going to be pissed when she found out. Kenzie could deal with it as long as she had her sister.

"Sounds good." He didn't let her go.

They were standing like that when the door slammed open and Jaek marched in, bearing a giant club that made him look like a barbarian caveman. "Where is she?" he demanded.

"Don't you have guards anymore?" Kenzie muttered. She didn't pull away quickly. She'd taken off her weapons when she was sitting with her sister, and she'd felt so safe that she hadn't bothered to put them back on. She carefully grabbed one of the throwing knives still on Mad's belt and concealed it in her hand.

Mad had to feel what she was doing, but he didn't stop her. And since Jaek was his friend, she didn't immediately throw the knife.

Relationships required compromise.

"She's sleeping," Kenzie said. No need to tell the guy about the supplement. "And she's okay. Thank you for taking care of her." She had to choke out that last part, but she'd seen the way her sister blushed when talking about Jaek. This man—alien—hadn't hurt Carise.

But it was probably good to get her sister away from him anyway.

"I want to see her." Jaek stomped further into the room, and his grip tightened on the club. He was ready to bust heads, but all the heads had been busted.

For now.

"You can't," Mad said. He stepped half a step in front of Kenzie, blocking Jaek from getting to her. "Come in the morning. Or stay here tonight and see her in the morning. Either is acceptable. But Carise needs her sleep."

Jaek's chest heaved, and Kenzie didn't have much hope of him seeing reason.

She hated when she was right.

He jabbed the end of the club at Mad, bumping against his chest, not to do any damage but rather to emphasize the point. "I want to see her now," he demanded. "I won't wake her up." He tried to pass by Mad.

Kenzie backed up and got between Jaek and the door that led to Carise's room. "Not going to happen today." The knife wouldn't do much damage to Jaek, not unless she got lucky. She *really* didn't want to fight him, and only a tiny bit of that had to do with him being Mad's friend. The guy was huge and she didn't think she could win.

But she wasn't letting a rampaging alien criminal go to her defenseless sister.

Something shifted in Jaek's eyes, and Kenzie knew things had just gone from bad to worse. He dropped the club and charged at her. Kenzie backed up, trying to get to the hallway and a door she could put in between her and Jaek before he got to her or to Carise.

Mad let out a furious scream and charged Jaek, tackling him to the hard stone floor and punching him across the jaw. It only took two hits for him to stay down.

Mad got up, knuckles raw and face a wash of anger. "Get out," he snapped through gritted teeth.

Jaek's eye was starting to darken with a bruise. "Mad—"

"You tried to hurt my mate." He leaned in close, and for a moment, Kenzie worried he would do something unforgivable. But he only scowled. "Get out of my territory until you learn some manners."

Something must have told Jaek that Mad meant business. Whether it was the mate thing or the absolute fury in Mad's voice, she wasn't sure.

And she didn't know how to feel when he called her his mate. She loved it. And it made her want to cry. But if she never cried again, it would be soon enough. She hated the way tears hollowed her out.

Why couldn't she just have one good thing? She couldn't ask Carise to stay here so Kenzie could have Mad. She couldn't ask Mad to leave so she could care for her sister.

She was stuck in between.

Jaek snatched up his club and left with a glare, a string of curses echoing from his mouth.

Mad's chest heaved. "I'll end him for this."

Okay. *That* was getting out of hand. She stood in front of Mad and placed her hand over his heart. He immediately covered her hand with his own. "Jaek is your friend and you're going to remember that tomorrow. I would have done the exact same thing, and nothing would get me to leave."

She wasn't sure if that made Jaek a more reasonable person. Or maybe he just trusted Mad enough.

"He tried to hurt you." Mad tightened his grip on her hand. "It's my job to protect you."

She held up the knife and waved it before carefully sliding it back into the sheath on Mad's belt. "I can take care of myself."

He made a feral noise that shouldn't have made her shiver with want. "I need to protect my mate. I've bonded you, but I haven't claimed you." The words were getting harsher by the second.

Really, this should not have been turning Kenzie

on. She'd seen Mad kill a man in this room only a few hours before.

And yet.

She kissed him fiercely and then pulled back. "I'm your mate. Claim me."

CHAPTER 29

Emotions swirled within Mad, and he'd never been more on edge. They stood in *his* throne room in *his* palace.

Kenzie was his mate. His fated mate.

This was no bond formed out of a desperate need for the energy that flowed between them. This was something formed by fate and decreed by the universe. And Mad needed his woman to understand exactly where they stood.

This was his palace.

But she was his queen.

He scooped her up in his arms and strode across the room until he seated her on his throne. She deserved a throne of her own right beside his, but that was a problem for a later day. He refused to be here without her. He wouldn't reign alone.

"Mad," Kenzie said before he knelt at her feet and ran his hands over her legs. "Fuck." She breathed it out.

Fuck yes. He needed this. They both needed this. It was time to feast.

Kenzie wore a dress right now, pale blue and nearly translucent in places. He didn't know where she'd gotten it but he wanted to find her a dozen more. Another part of him wanted to burn it. The dress showed off his mate to the world, and a violent, possessive part wanted to keep her only for himself.

He growled, and Kenzie put a hand on his shoulder. "You doing okay there, big guy?" she asked in a tone a person might use with an animal.

There was a sea inside of him, waves crashing violently against the shore and demanding he take action, that he take his mate. "More than fine," he told her, the words low, a dark promise.

Her legs fell open, just enough for him to trace his hands over her naked thighs and hike her skirt up until she was bared for him. She wore nothing under the dress, an unbearable temptation.

His cock threatened to burst out of his leathers, and he refused to touch it. Not now, not yet. He would bury himself deep inside of her until he forgot where he ended and she began, but first he had to feast.

He laid kisses on her thighs, first on top and then making his way inside and teasing her tender flesh. She shivered and didn't resist as he looped her legs over his shoulders and opened her fully to him.

He couldn't get enough of her taste on his tongue, earthly and womanly and everything he wanted. He could stay here for days, his tongue and lips bringing her more pleasure than he ever imagined he knew how to give.

And when her fingers dug into his scalp, he groaned. He wanted her to hold him there and use him, to take her pleasure as a queen should when her subject knelt at her feet. She was wet around him, her arousal growing with every lap of his tongue. But Mad refused to pull away until she screamed his name.

This was their coronation. He might have defeated the former king and taken the palace, but right now he was truly becoming king.

Kenzie's hips bucked and she cried out his name as the first orgasm took her, and Mad felt masculine satisfaction at bringing her over that wave. But he wanted more. He wanted her clinging to him with lust until she forgot everything except the heat between them.

He didn't let up, and she begged him for more.

He had to reach down and free himself from his own leathers, undoing the string that held them in place and shoving his pants down. If he touched himself, this would all be over, but having his cock free to the air was its own kind of torture.

A torture he would gladly endure so long as his mate took her pleasure from his tongue.

She did, coming again, even harder this time.

And Mad could take no more. He had to be inside her. Now.

He surged up and took her with him, seating himself on the throne and taking her down to his lap. Her pupils were blown wide with pleasure, her bottom lip swollen from where she must have bit it to keep from crying out.

He wanted her sounds. He wanted everything from her.

She slid down onto him slowly, her face a wash of pleasure as her tight heat enveloped him. Mad buried his face in the crook of her neck, groaning out a noise as the slow press of her body nearly undid him. It was too much. Too, too much.

And yet there was more.

Her body swallowed him fully until he was seated deep inside of her, right where he belonged.

The mate bond flared between them, energy rushing into him and growing within her. He didn't know how humans did it or quite how the mate bond functioned to allow him to pull energy from Kenzie without harming her.

Right now, it didn't matter. All that mattered was the physical bond between them.

She moved, riding him like some sort of wild creature, her body sliding against his. Mad clutched her hips and thrust up with her, their bodies moving together. It was fast and wet and perfect.

And he had to use every ounce of discipline he'd ever learned to keep from spilling himself right then, it felt so good.

But he hung on.

Kenzie arched her head back, bearing her throat fully, a moan coming from deep in her throat. Mad laid kisses all along her sensitive skin and watched as a flush crawled over her.

Stars above, she was magnificent.

And all his.

Her moan turned into a gasp, and her body shuddered around his, clutching him tight in its grasp. And he was undone, shooting into her as his own release found him.

Kenzie shuddered against him and leaned

forward, giving him all of her weight like some kind of puppet whose strings had been cut. He wrapped his arms around her and held her there.

"Holy shit," she mumbled into his ear, placing a clumsy kiss somewhere between his chin and his neck.

Humans had the funniest sayings. But now wasn't the time to dwell on that. Mad couldn't make himself let go of his mate. He leaned back against the plush back of the throne and kept her with him.

"There were many things I thought I might do in Jadirel's throne room," Mad mused, running one hand up and down Kenzie's back, "but I never imagined this." Somehow, she was still mostly clothed, her dress bunched up around her waist. He needed to find a place for them to sleep for the night.

"Don't ruin the afterglow by saying that asshole's name," she said. "It's your throne room now. Never thought I'd fuck a king."

"Before everything else, I am your mate." The joy and satisfaction that went through him at that realization was enough to re-energize him for another round.

"In a bed next time, mate," Kenzie teased, giving him a kiss before pulling back. "I bet there's a nice big bath somewhere in here. And a nice big bed.

Let's go find it." She grabbed his hand and tugged him off the throne.

Mad had to let go to fix his pants, which he did with a wry smile. And then he followed his mate, just as fate intended.

29

MAD REFUSED TO SLEEP IN JADIREL'S OLD BED. IT WAS A matter of principle. But the palace was big enough that he'd been able to take a different room for himself and Kenzie, and something in his chest unfurled when he woke up with his mate curled up beside him.

Light streamed in through a large window. The room smelled pleasantly of some kind of perfume. It was warm and clean and as perfect as things got on Guerran.

Every morning should be like this.

But how?

He'd only been up for thirty seconds when the weight of everything he'd done the day before crashed down on him. He'd killed Jadirel and taken his territory. *He* was an exile king.

And he had a mate.

There were a hundred, maybe a thousand, things he should do. He had to figure out what exactly went into running a territory on Guerran.

If that was what he was going to do.

Kenzie was relaxed in sleep, and some of the years had cleared from her face. She didn't look young, exactly, but she was unburdened. She'd done her job, she'd found her sister. And now she could do whatever she wanted with the future.

Did that include him?

Becoming an exile king was an accident of necessity. And there were certainly things he could fix in the territory now that Jadirel was gone. He had to make sure there were no more slaves in the palace, and he was going to kick the slavers out of the territory. Maybe it wouldn't last if he didn't stick around, but he had to do at least that.

Hard as it was to believe, he still had time to catch the ride off the planet that Arbyn had arranged for him. Perhaps there would be two seats for Kenzie and Carise as well. Though Jaek might forcibly board the ship to see Carise if he didn't see her before they left.

If the mating bond had sparked in Jaek, Mad understand his urge. He *couldn't* let Kenzie go, not if she would have him, not if she would allow him to love her. He'd merely been existing on Guerran until she burst into his life. For the first time in six years, he felt like he might actually have a future.

And yet that future was so precarious he felt like he was strung on a high wire and at risk of toppling over at any minute.

Kenzie made a little noise and turned over, opening her eyes and looking at him. "Good morning."

He smiled at her. "Good morning. Especially since you're not touching a knife."

She rolled her eyes and shuffled up into a sitting position beside him, completely heedless of her nudity. "Killing kings is your job. Besides, my knife is right there." She nodded towards the bedside table.

"Queens shouldn't kill their kings." It sounded absurd. Mad was no king. And yet he'd slept the night in a palace. He'd taken Jadirel's territory. It could all be his.

If.

"So I'm your queen now?" He couldn't easily interpret the tone of Kenzie's voice. Was that sadness? Regret?

"Only if you want to be." Mad pulled her close. They'd slept the night together, but right now he needed to be touching her, needed to remind himself that they'd survived the impossible. Now all they had to do was take their lives into their own hands and live as they wished. "*Do* you want to be my queen?"

"I'm no queen," Kenzie scoffed. But everything about her was regal in his eyes, no need for a crown. He wanted one for her anyway. She deserved to be draped in jewels and finery.

"You're my mate. No one else will ever sit at my side."

If anything, that made it worse. She stiffened and pulled away from him, sliding out of the bed and pulling on her clothes. "Mad—" She didn't say anything more.

But he knew. He'd been trying not to think of it ever since the sisters were reunited. "It's Carise, isn't it?" His heart was heavy with the question, but he understood Kenzie's love for her sister. How could he not? He knew what it meant to be an older sibling.

For half a second, Kenzie looked wrecked, eyes on the verge of tears, mouth open to let out an anguished cry. But she pulled it all back until her face was blank. "I've been looking for her for *years*. I'm her big sister. I have to protect her. I can't ask her to stay on a planet where she was a *slave*. She'll never be able to heal."

Mad wrapped Kenzie in his arms. He didn't want

her hiding her emotions, not from him, not when they were alone together. "We don't have to stay here."

Saying it was a punch to his gut. Flying away from Guerran meant giving up every chance he had of seeing his own family again. He wouldn't even be able to call them. At most he might be able to relay a letter to Taiana every year or so. Would she even write him back?

Would Derok remember who he was?

It hurt to think it. But it hurt even more to think of giving up his mate. Kenzie was his future, not some hope for a pardon that would probably never come. Kenzie was real and right there. He had to be strong for her.

He had to give her this future.

"We?" The tears had started to fall now, but she wasn't hiding from him anymore.

He kissed her quickly and pulled back before passion could sweep them away in its tide. "You're my mate. If we go, we go together."

"But your family." She understood. It tempered the hurt. Kenzie knew what it was to love family. She knew what it was to go anywhere to find them, just as he'd endured anything for the hope of reunification.

He couldn't put it into words easily. How could

he explain all the jumbled up emotions inside of him? If he said he was doing it solely for her, she'd never let him get away with it. He knew his mate too well for that.

Before he could say anything, there was an insistent knock at the door. He and Kenzie looked at each other in confusion.

"Were you expecting anyone?" she asked.

"Why do I have a feeling this is part of king life?" He pulled on the rest of his clothes and made sure Kenzie was mostly covered before yanking the door open and barking at the guard. "What?"

The guard shrank back. He wore rumpled clothing and didn't look as if he'd slept all night. What had Jadirel been doing to these men that they feared a strong word? Mad would need to go through the ranks and figure out who he could trust and—well, maybe not. Not if he, Kenzie, and Carise were about to leave Guerran.

"What?" he repeated when the guard sputtered. He didn't have time for this when he and Kenzie were in the middle of deciding the rest of their lives.

The guard took a steadying breath and managed to meet his eyes. "It's Carise, sire. She's gone."

30

Kenzie heard the guard's words and her heart stopped. Then she sprang into motion, sprinting past Mad and down the hall to where Carise was supposed to be safe.

Gone?

Gone!

How?

Kenzie wanted to scream. She wanted to cut the answers out of people until she knew exactly where Carise was and whether or not she was safe. Had someone abducted her in the night?

Had one of the guards been so loyal to Jadirel that he'd taken Carise away to where other people would hurt her?

Had Kenzie had her in her grasp only to lose her because she was so selfish that she'd rather fuck a hot alien than sit vigil at her sister's side? Only when her fingers closed around hard wood did she realize she had a knife in her hands.

She had to calm down. She couldn't tear through the palace in a rage looking for evidence of where her sister was. She needed to do it methodically, to gather every bit of evidence and chase down whoever dared to put a finger on Carise.

Was it Jaek?

She could take Jaek. None of her previous doubts mattered.

"She can't have gone far." Kenzie barely recognized her own voice. "I need to find her."

Mad was right beside her, and he put a hand on her shoulder. "I think you should read this first." He handed her a folded piece of paper. "It was on Carise's pillow."

"Ransom?" Kenzie didn't have much money, but that didn't matter. Ransom meant that Carise was probably alive.

"Just read the note." Mad sounded... strange.

She met his eyes and saw concern. "I'm fine," she tried to assure him. The fact that she had to grit it out through clenched teeth didn't help her cause. She unfolded the paper and read.

Dear Kenzie,

I'm sorry for leaving like this. I'm safe and with a

friend. I know that's not going to stop you worrying about me, so I promise that I will send a note to check in at least once a week.

Thank you so much for coming for me. I knew you would. Even in the darkest days, I knew my big sister would come. That hope kept me alive when nothing else would. And you came! You freed me! I was so happy to see you and I love you so much.

But I need to figure things out for me. You were making so many plans last night that I didn't have time to get a word in edgewise. I don't want to go back to Earth, at least not yet. And it's not about Jaek, I promise. He ALSO kept me safe for a little while, but that's not it.

This is about me.

For the first time in years, I have my freedom. I want to figure out who I am and what I want. And I'm afraid that if I leave here with you, I'm not going to be able to do that. You're a little overprotective, okay?

I'm a big girl now. Let me figure out how to take care of myself.

This isn't goodbye AT ALL. We're going to see each other again and we're going to be sisters. But I need my time. Please give it to me.

I will always love you. I will always be your little sister.

But let me figure out who I am now.

-Carise

The letter was a punch to the gut, and Kenzie stumbled back until she was sitting on Carise's perfectly made bed. She wordlessly handed the letter to Mad, who scanned it with a serious look on his face.

"How did she leave?" he asked, and Kenzie was about to give a sharp response when she realized he was talking to a guard.

She looked up and glared at the guard, who shrank back, but steeled himself and responded anyway. "She walked out on her own about an hour ago," the guard reported. "She had breakfast delivered shortly before sunrise and ate it all. Then she requested new clothing and paper. She asked the attendant if she was allowed to go for a walk, and the attendant told her she was not a prisoner here, so she could do whatever she pleased. She left shortly after that, and when the attendant realized she had been gone for so long, the guard was notified. I have the attendant in the cell awaiting punishment, sire."

"What?" Mad startled, and even Kenzie was taken aback, no matter her previous desire for violence. "The attendant was doing their job. No punishment necessary. Let them go."

"But the girl escaped!" the guard sputtered.

"She wasn't a prisoner." Kenzie said it faintly, but

she had to make herself believe it. Carise *wasn't* a prisoner. She was free to walk away whenever she wanted.

"Leave us," Mad told the guard.

When they were alone in Carise's room, he gathered Kenzie in a tight hug. "We can still go after her," he said. "If she's only been gone an hour, she can't have gotten far."

Kenzie wanted to. So bad. It was on the tip of her tongue to agree with Mad's suggestion. "Give me the letter, please." Mad did, and Kenzie read it again. The words hadn't magically changed. "I don't know what I said last night, but I scared her. I can't chase after her. She'll just keep running. Guerran may not be the safest place in the galaxy, but she's *here* and I know it. And she's free. If she needs time to figure herself out, then I won't chase after her."

"Do you think she went to Jaek?" he asked quietly.

She shook her head. "She implies she didn't. But we can always hunt him down if we think otherwise."

"As long as she's in my territory, she's safe," Mad vowed.

Despite the situation, Kenzie's lips curved into a smile. "Your territory? You're getting used to the whole exile king thing."

Mad pulled her close and kissed her. "As long as you are here, I will protect you. I will *always* stay by your side. Will you be my queen?"

Kenzie could say yes and have almost everything she wanted. The situation with her sister was rocky, but that could improve. And she could keep Mad. It wasn't the future she'd imagined for herself, back when she'd been capable of imagining a future, but it was hers.

And yet she remembered the conversation they'd been having right before they discovered Carise had left.

"What do *you* want, Mad? Before you were talking as if you were ready to leave. Now you're staying because I'm staying. What if one day I want to leave? We *just* met. This is crazy." Crazy how right it felt, at least. Kenzie's heart had been breaking at the thought of walking away, but how could she just accept this?

Mad kissed her again, but when he pulled away, his face was serious. "You are my mate." He kissed her again. "My place is at your side, wherever that may be." He traced his hand down her cheek. "On Guerran, off Guerran, it doesn't matter. I want to see my own family again, but there's no guarantee of that, there never was. But with you, I can build something of my own, of our own. Be my mate. Be my lover. Be my queen."

There was only so much her heart could take before bursting with happiness. She was balancing on a wire, her emotions teetering between despair and joy. She had Mad. She had *this*.

And she wasn't letting him go.

She grabbed Mad's hand and laced their fingers together. "Let's go figure out how to run a kingdom."

EPILOGUE

CARISE WASN'T RUNNING. SHE'D LEARNED A LONG TIME ago that running was useless. They caught you quicker if you ran.

They caught you no matter what.

But if she could get far enough away from the godforsaken palace, maybe this time she'd have her freedom.

She'd been so unbelievably happy to see Kenzie that at first she'd known it *had* to be a hallucination. Good things didn't happen to her. Not anymore.

What about Jaek?

She banished the thought. She couldn't think about him right now. Not if she wanted to keep her sanity. She clutched the note in her pocket, kept her head down, and kept walking.

If she'd stayed, Kenzie would have taken control

of her life. She'd already been making plans and didn't pause to consider whether or not Carise wanted it. She couldn't go back to Earth. Kenzie didn't know what it was like, not really. She'd always carved a path for herself.

Carise took whatever path she could find.

She ducked into the shadows between two buildings and read the note again, just to reassure herself it was real. It didn't say much, just gave her the words to say to get out of the palace and an address she needed to go to.

It was signed *a friend.*

Was it Jaek?

Her heart started beating a little faster at the thought. But it wasn't like him, at least not as she'd gotten to know him over the last few weeks.

Was she being stupid?

She'd just been freed, and now she was running off because a note she'd found shoved under her pillow told her there was another path? She almost turned around right then and walked back to the palace.

Kenzie would forgive her. Eventually.

But she'd probably lock Carise up for her own safety for another two years.

Was she being uncharitable? Maybe. But Kenzie

hadn't even *asked* if Carise wanted to go back to Earth. If Carise went back, Kenzie would insist that she leave. She wouldn't understand why Carise wanted to stay.

Carise wasn't sure that *she* understood why she wanted to stay. But she had to. For now.

She checked the directions again and took off before her nerves could fail her. They brought her to a small cafe where a human woman was waiting at a table in the front of the room. She stood and smiled when Carise arrived.

"You got my note," she said.

Carise tried not to be disappointed that Jaek hadn't left the note, even though that was impossible.

"How?" That had been another thing. Clearly the palace wasn't safe if someone could just slip into a room and put notes under a person's bed. Carise wanted to know if there was any trouble.

The woman's smile got even wider. "I have my ways. My name is Layala. I know your sister. I helped her find you."

"Oh."

Layala motioned for her to sit and poured tea from a teapot sitting on the table. "Please, have a seat, and some tea."

Carise sat. Layala had a way of speaking that

made Carise want to do whatever she said. She took the tea and sipped.

Layala poured her own tea from the same pot and sipped, savoring it. "I'm glad you came to see me."

"Why?" Carise didn't like it when people wanted her. That never turned out well.

But Layala said something she didn't expect.

"I'd like to offer you a job."

———

Thank you for reading *Exile's Hunter*!
I'd appreciate it so much if you would consider leaving a review.

The series will continue with Carise's book!

WHAT'S TO READ NEXT:
SYNNR'S SAINT

Taken from Earth and used like a lab rat...

Emily was a normal law student until she was abducted by aliens. Forced to perform death defying feats by night and undergoing medical tests by day, she doesn't know how much longer she can take it. When one alien takes particular interest in her she's afraid things have gone from bad to worse. He's got wings and fangs, and he makes her heart pound. But she can't want an alien like that... can she?

He doesn't have time to rescue a human...

Oz is on Kilrym for a reason, and it's not to rescue the ethereal performer who captivates him by night. But covert ops are impossible when his mind is on the human who could be his fated mate. War is on the horizon, but what if the only way to save his people is to sacrifice Emily?

Despite the fact that they were born light years apart, they are a perfect match. But Oz is keeping secrets, and when Emily finds out the truth she may never be able to forgive him, no matter how much she needs him to survive and escape the planet alive.

ALSO BY KATE RUDOLPH

Looking for something else? Kate Rudolph has a heart pounding collection or paranormal and sci-fi romance stories for you! Bundles, bears, audiobooks, aliens, and more. Check out your options in the list below. You can find out all you need to know at www.katerudolph.net.

Want to check out one of the books? Click on the series name to find out more!

Dragon Brides

Fated mates, fierce women, and dragon princes.

Crux

Ranger

Saber

Alien Mates: Planet Exile

Guerran is no place for pretty human women. But these alien heroes will protect their mates!

Christmas... in space????

These alien holiday romances look beyond Earth's winter holidays and ring in the season across the galaxy! ***Select titles available in audio.***

Snowed in with the Alien Beast

The Alien's Winter Gift

The Alien Reindeer's Wild Ride

Trapped with her Alien Mate

———

Alien Outlaws

Outlaws, schemes, and love... it's all there in the Alien Outlaws series...

Andie Munster is sick of life on Ixilta, the planet she got dumped on after being abducted from Earth six years ago. And when the mysterious and dangerous Xandr shows up looking for a way off the planet, she's half-prisoner, half-co-conspirator in a wild rush to escape.

Rogue Alien's Escape

Rogue Alien's Woman

Rogue Alien's Secret

Rogue Alien's Legacy

———

Mated to the Alien

Fated Mate Alien Romance

Detyens are doomed to die young if they don't find their fated mates.

Follow along as these mated pairs fight off aliens, corrupt dictators, prejudiced humans, pirates, and more! The books can be read or listened to in any order, though some characters show up in multiple stories.

Select books available in audio.

Pick a book and jump into the action today!

Ruwen

Tyral

Stoan

Cyborg

Krayter

Kayleb

Shayn

Braxtyn

Doryan

Dekon

———

Stealing the Alpha

The thief takes what she wants, but the alpha keeps what's his...

Join shifter thief Mel as she clashes with lion alpha Luke in an explosive trilogy of two opposites who can't keep away from one another.

Also available in audio!

The Alpha Heist

Entangled with the Thief

In the Alpha's Bed

Save with box sets!

Aliens. Shifters. Warriors. Mates. Get them all wrapped together in these special box sets. Save up to 30% off the price of buying the individual books, depending on the series!

Alien Outlaws: The Complete Series

Mated to the Alien Volume One (also available in audio)

Mated to the Alien Volume Two (also available in audio)

Mated to the Alien Volume Three

Mated to the Alien Volume Four

Stealing the Alpha: The Complete Series (also available in audio)

The Mate Bundle

Detyen Warriors Volume One (also available in audio)

Detyen Warriors Volume Two (also available in audio)

Zulir Warrior Mates Volume One (also available in audio)

———

Standalone Paranormal and Sci-Fi Romance:

Crashed

Mated on the Moon

Mated to the Alien Dragon

Marked

Bear in Mind

Alpha's Mercy

Gemma's Mate

Find more by Kate Rudolph at www.katerudolph.net

ABOUT KATE RUDOLPH

Kate Rudolph is a paranormal and alien romance author who lives in Indiana. She loves writing about kick butt heroines and the steamy heroes who love them. She's been devouring romance novels since she was too young to be reading them and had to hide her books so no one would take them away. She couldn't imagine a better job in this world than writing romances and sharing them with her fellow readers.

If you enjoyed this story, please consider leaving a review.